The Path to True Love

by

Karen Stanley

Raven Crest Books

RAVEN CREST
BOOKS

Publishing the best in new literary voices

Cover Design by www.StunningBookCovers.com

ISBN: 978-1-9997803-3-3

THE PATH TO TRUE LOVE

Amber remembered the day vividly when she first set eyes on Jamie Truelove. He had been the talk of the school, arriving part way through Year 10, resplendent in his stay-press trousers, waffle cardigan and moccasins. He had one of those 'quiffy' kind of hairstyles that she was pretty sure only stayed in place due to a large quantity of his Mum's 'Silvikrin Extra Firm hold,' and he *oozed* cool. The kind of cool that is only evident to a bunch of 15-year-old boys, with barely disguised acne and voices that squeak with embarrassing unpredictability, and their fawning female counterparts, *obviously*…but cool nevertheless. Amber and her friends would hang around outside the school gates, or in their form rooms, waiting expectantly for a glimpse of the object of their affections, and the chance to blush furiously and open and close their mouths like a ventriloquist's dummy if Jamie and his mates even deigned to look their way – let alone speak to them. They would run off, giggling uncontrollably in the way only teenage girls can, before dissecting, discussing and analysing the whole brief encounter for hours on the phone later that evening.

Throughout the remainder of her school years, Amber could only dream of anything like a proper date with the wonderful Jamie, in fact she was sure he had barely even noticed her existence amongst the gaggle of near-hysterical admirers who seemed to follow in his wake. Her and Jamie's 'relationship' was merely a figment of Amber's imagination – long nights where she lay awake in her bed fantasising about him finally asking her out and kissing her passionately in the back seat of the cinema. She wasn't altogether sure what 'kissing passionately' exactly entailed, but she was sure that a man of the world such as Jamie would be experienced enough to show her. She took to watching pop videos and soppy movies where the girl got thoroughly kissed at the end, and practising her technique on the back of her hand.

Eventually, Jamie and his mates left to join various YTS schemes, being 'far too cool for school' by this point, and Amber and her more sensible (and undeniably square) friends stayed on to pursue worthwhile educational studies such as 'A' levels in Food and Nutrition, and Media Studies. It was a year after finishing her own schooling, and now working on the make-up counter in Boots, having been unable to find any high-powered jobs that combined being able to make a jam Swiss roll and knowing about the explosion of digital communication technology in the late 20th century, that she once again bumped into Jamie.

More accurately, *he* bumped into *her* just as she was rushing back late, again, from her lunch break. She had hurtled through the revolving doors clutching a half-eaten prawn sandwich and a half-finished chocolate milk shake, just he was leaving the store, reading his paper and totally not looking where he was going. They had inevitably collided and, resisting the urge to scream, 'Watch where you're fucking going!' (she did work here, after all, and she really needed this job) Amber barely looked up as she tried to rub the splatter of ice cold milk shake that had landed inappropriately on her left breast, the nipple of which was now protruding shamelessly. The sound of Jamie's voice exclaiming, "Bloody hell, if it isn't little Amber Nectar!" distracted her from openly groping her own breast and she looked up, her eyes meeting his directly. Well, they would have met his directly, if he hadn't been blatantly ogling her erect nipple which was now even more visible due to the large, cold, wet patch covering it!

Amber recognised him immediately and, alarmingly, reverted to a 15-year-old stuttering, blushing schoolgirl, seemingly incapable of stringing even two coherent words together.

"Lovely to see you again," grinned Jamie, his eyes meeting hers briefly, before indiscreetly returning to ogle her tits.

Amber blushed again and tried to cross her arms awkwardly in an attempt to hide her exposed lady bits.

"You've grown," smiled Jamie with a cheeky wink, clearly enjoying her embarrassment.

Amber squirmed a little more. "Oh, er, hi! Yes. So have you," she replied, inwardly kicking herself at her seriously shit reply.

Jamie continued to gaze at her with a wry smile. "So, what's a nice girl like you doing in a place like this?"

"I, er… I, erm… I….Anyway, what did you call me?" Amber would have bet money that Jamie didn't even know her name, let alone have a nickname for her!

"Amber Nectar," smiled Jamie, "As in nectar, you know; a bit of a honey!" He at least had the good grace to blush himself as he said this, but only slightly, and his cool demeanor was quickly restored. He was still annoyingly good looking –more so, if that was possible. The teenage spots had been replaced by a very mature smattering of stubble and his dark quiffy hair was now gelled in the messy 'just got out of bed look' which actually probably took ages!

If Amber had been struggling for words before, she was now positively mute and continued to stand in front of him, blushing furiously and looking like she had entered a wet t-shirt competition.

After a couple more excruciating minutes, during which Jamie seemed to positively revel in her awkwardness, Amber managed to somehow make her excuses and make her way back to the counter where she worked, ignoring the icy stare of her slightly senior colleague (and therefore self-appointed boss), and never so grateful for the hideous tabard that they were forced to wear during work hours.

Normally she avoided having to wear the lilac monstrosity like the plague but, sporting as she was, one wet, stained, and still brazenly erect breast, she was very grateful for its coverage – lilac or otherwise.

After that, Jamie seemed to 'pop in' to Boots more and more. Once, he shamelessly winked at her whilst buying a pack of lager flavoured condoms, which he later confessed he only did to wind her up and because she looked so sexy when she blushed – bastard!

Eventually he nonchalantly asked her if she'd like to go out for a drink with him and she tried, and failed, to answer as she had never even considered the possibility – let alone woken in the night dreaming about it and with her hand mysteriously tucked inside her knickers!

He picked her up that evening in his red Mark V Cortina, complete with fake walnut dash and leatherette seats – he was still so cool! They went to the pictures and snogged furiously in the back row and, once again, she awoke in the night, very flushed and with her hand back inside her knickers!

She tried to resist his advances for about as long as she could, which basically amounted to about 3 weeks, partly because she didn't want him to think she was a slag, and mainly because she was still a virgin and because she was pretty bloody certain he wasn't! She knew she wanted him, she just wasn't sure how to go about it – it was all very well watching re-runs of Dirty Dancing, and she was sure she could do the back-arching and sultry eyes half-closed during the crucial bit, she just wasn't sure she knew what the crucial bit *actually* entailed. Of course she had taken biology at 'O' Level but that was really only the mechanics without the sultry stuff. She had considered renting a porn video for a bit of research, but the only place she knew that did under-the-counter rentals was Ron's corner shop up the road, and she also knew that her dad shared a pint with Ron at the local social club on a Saturday night, so that was totally out of the question!

When the time came, Jamie was quite sweet about the whole thing and she suspected he wasn't quite as experienced as he'd have had her believe – although he still knew a damn sight more than she did. He was secretly pleased that he was her first, although it made him more cock-sure than usual – in more ways than one!

The whole thing wasn't quite as earth-shattering as she'd hoped and she struggled to really see what the fuss was about, but she guessed she'd get the hang of it eventually. There wasn't a great deal of foreplay apart from a lot of snogging and a quick fumble in her knickers, after which it was all over fairly quickly. The nighttime throbbing in her nether regions was replaced by a throbbing of a more uncomfortable kind that thankfully subsided in a few days - after which it was business as usual.

As time progressed they spent more and more time together before they finally got engaged. Amber had been delighted that he'd asked her and felt terribly 'grown up' at the prospect of being someone's fiancée. Their wedding was a couple of years later; Jamie wore a double-breasted suit with a red carnation buttonhole and she wore something white and frilly that made her resemble a cross between a meringue and one of those toilet roll covers in the shape of a doll like her Grandma used to have. She'd had a wreath of artificial red and white roses plonked on her head, her curly permed fringe poking out from underneath, and white stilettos that gave her blisters. Predictably, having married her 'Truelove', the jokes about finding the path to True Love would follow her throughout her married life – something which at first was sweet but eventually grew quite tiring, especially if Jamie was being a bit of a twat!

They hadn't been able to afford a honeymoon so had spent a wet week in Jamie's nan's caravan in Margate – hardly Barbados or the Seychelles! Amber remembered vividly spending an afternoon with Jamie's uncle in their caravan on the same site. The whole family had come down for the day to celebrate Jamie and Amber's recent nuptials. Jamie's uncle owned a hotel in Margate and was therefore the 'tycoon' of the family – revered by all because of his detached house and 2.8 litre injection Ford Capri. They spent a dull afternoon in his caravan listening to him wax lyrical about his 'self-made' success before going for a carvery in the local Beefeater. Amber was pretty surprised when Jamie's cousin produced a calculator at the end of the meal to work out the bill because she worked in a bank. She proceeded to dissect the bill, item by item, figuring out who'd had the extra tonic water and the garlic mushrooms. The bill had come to about £170 for all 18 of them in total. After twenty minutes of Cousin Sarah furiously working away on her calculator, Amber had just about had enough. "Why don't we all just put in a tenner and that includes a tip for the waitress instead of fussing about the odd 20p here and there?" she'd suggested, albeit admittedly in a loud and less than patient tone. (They should have considered themselves lucky that she hadn't started her question with…'for fuck's sake!')

An awkward silence descended upon the whole group and Cousin Sarah huffily stuffed her calculator back into her organiser handbag. Amber had received a sharp kick in the ankles from Jamie whilst family members, now too embarrassed to protest, reluctantly placed their tenners into the plate in the middle of the table. Amber had received a sympathetic 'thank you' gaze from Jamie's auntie Winnie, but then she'd had the extra tonic water, the garlic mushrooms AND a Tia Maria coffee!

That night, she and Jamie had barely spoken and she had laid in her bed in the caravan wondering why he hadn't at least stood up for her – bloody Patrick Swayze aka Johnny had managed it for Baby!

He'd sulked for most of the next day but had finally relented when she'd promised him a blow job – anything for a quiet life! To add insult to injury, on the day before they left, a slip of paper had been pushed under their door detailing the cost of the pint of Fosters and two gin and tonics they'd drunk in his uncle's caravan before 'Carvery-gate!' His bloody uncle had sent them a bill! No wonder he had a detached house and a Capri – tight-fisted bastard!

After their honeymoon, they rented a flat above a restaurant and lived there fairly happily until Jamie's nan died and left them enough money for a deposit on a two-up, two-down up the road from his Mum's house. Jamie was a hard worker, if nothing else, and they were reasonably comfortable, if not rich. Amber continued to work at Boots – unfulfilled, but too apathetic to do anything else.

Eventually, Jamie started his own building firm and began to do pretty well. They moved to a larger house, and had two children. Amber continued to work at Boots – if only part-time now – and Jamie's mum had the children. Jamie's mum, June, was a forceful woman whose kindness was often merely a mask to disguise her over-whelming need to poke her bloody nose into absolutely everything! Sure, she was good to the kids, but Amber got sick of her little jibes - 'Daniel says you don't normally give him breakfast,' or 'Holly says her shoes are hurting her feet…' Yeah, well, Daniel and Holly are 6 and 8 and therefore will pretty much say bloody anything if it means they get an extra bowl of coco-pops or a new pair of sandals!

Amber learned to ignore June, the same as she learned to ignore Jamie when he was being an arse. As time had gone on, they had settled into comfortable normality. The kids were now grown up and off to university or travelling around the world, and she and Jamie were comfortably off. They got along pretty well most of the time – as long as his pants were washed and he didn't have to raise a bloody finger around the house! On the rare occasion when he did cook her a meal or empty the dishwasher (that is removing the ***one*** plate he needed from the clean crockery in the dishwasher and leaving the others in there!) he expected a fanfare and a round of sodding applause. No-one played the fucking trumpet when she brought the washing in, did they?!

They had sex most Saturdays and usually it was ok. No rose petals or strings playing in the distance – but ok. She was usually fairly well satisfied and, if they did it early enough, she got to settle down with a good book afterwards before she went to sleep.

Her books were Amber's solace. She loved to read what Jamie called 'housewife porn'. Truth be told, it wasn't so much the sex bit she liked as much as the romance. She didn't really understand how you could do it five times in one night with a whole host of gadgets buzzing in your knickers and still be up for more. For a start, she couldn't imagine getting up for work when you'd only had about 30 minutes sleep and your lady parts were chafed to buggery and pouting like a codfish! And, really, who would be 'panting for more as he denied her orgasm over and over?' More like, telling the bastard to get on with it before you punched him in the face and finished the job yourself!

No, Amber just loved the hearts and flowers. She wanted to be whisked away to Paris on a surprise trip by a man who had packed a picnic lunch of strawberries and champagne, she wanted rose petals and floating candles in her bath, she wanted breakfast in bed and maybe just a bit of great sex. The kind of sex that made your toes curl, the kind of sex that made her wet with anticipation brought on by a man who got a hard-on every time he was alone in lift with her.

She remembered she and Jamie had tried the odd sexual adventure over the years but it was never accompanied with strawberries and champagne. They did once try, 'eating food off your partner's body', (as suggested by Cosmopolitan) but the only thing they'd had in the fridge that was remotely suitable was some leftover tiramisu which, although tasty, had left a terrible mess on the sheets and had caused their pubes to stick together which was actually quite painful! Jamie had tried to persuade her that 'women loved to have their bum holes massaged', but Amber was not having any of it and felt distinctly uncomfortable about anyone going anywhere near that part of her body. She wasn't altogether sure how Jamie knew that women 'loved' this kind of thing, but guessed it was probably 'tits and tyres' talk amongst him and his mates down the pub. The kind of talk where they all bullshit each other about how much shagging they do, how many blow jobs they get and how big their willies are!

So, for now, Amber would just have to make do with their Saturday night ritual of: a little bit of cuddling, some snogging (as long as she'd cleaned her teeth), Jamie's fairly successful attempt at oral pleasure, followed by five minutes of shagging, where he usually liked her to get on top so he could ogle her tits while he came - (some things never changed!).

After which, she would read her book with the little light she'd bought on Amazon and fantasize about being whisked off to Rome in a billionaire's helicopter, before being tied up with a red silk tie and tickled with a sex toy that looked like a feather duster. After which she would, of course, be taken on the shopping trip to end all shopping trips, like Julia Roberts in Pretty Woman, before a final shag in the back of a limo on the way home (privacy screen behind the driver to be kept raised of course!)

Things would probably have bobbed along this way until she became too old to care about romance, or too blind to read her books. That was, of course, if she hadn't met Franc.

Amber didn't have a massive circle of close friends – she did have friends, of course, but over the years they had become more 'coupley' friends than just *her* friends. She was reasonably close to her mum, but her mum had been a bit older when she'd had Amber and so wasn't really mobile enough to enjoy long shopping trips or nights out that didn't include being in bed by 9. She didn't really want to chat to their mutual friends about her yearning for a bit of knee-trembling romance, and she wasn't sure her mum's heart could take the strain of discussing, 'how to lick chocolate off your partner's willy', with her daughter – besides, sex talk with your Mum? Wrong, on quite a few levels!

She had been sat on the sofa reading, whilst Jamie had flicked aimlessly through every sodding channel on the TV before settling on some crap about how to turn 'salvage' into art – aka making a really shit lamp out of a 'retro' petrol can that still looked like a rusty old petrol can – resisting the urge to smash him in the face, while he crunched his way through an entire family-sized bag of twiglets. How could one person make so much noise eating a bag of fucking crisps? He seemed to take ages; rustling the bloody bag every time he extracted one bloody twiglet at a time. Then crunch, crunch, crunch, followed by more rustling as he searched for yet another twiglet. The bag was like Mary Poppins' sodding carpet bag – bottomless! Amber squirmed in her seat as she tried to zone out the relentless crunching, biting her lip and trying really hard not to tell him to shut the fuck up! Eventually, when she could bear it no longer, she got out of her seat and offered him a cup of tea. Hopefully by the time she had made the tea he would have finished the bottomless bag of twiglets – or choked on them –whichever came sooner!

She returned to the lounge with two mugs of tea, thankful that his snacks did at last seem to be gone. She soon felt her irritation return as she then had to listen to him slurp his way through his cuppa, one excruciating, slow slurp at a time.

"For Christ's sake, it's like sitting next to a sodding horse!" she'd exclaimed.

"What you on about?" replied Jamie, slopping tea into his lap and all over her recently washed cushions.

Amber declined to answer. She didn't trust herself to

be nice – she wasn't sure she could rely on herself not to stab him to death with her nail scissors at that precise moment! She had got up and left the room, chucking her tea in the sink and making her way to the bedroom. She had intended to read a bit more of her latest book – 'Possessed by You' – the sequel to 'Captured by You', but she had become distracted by a post on Facebook about a local art group that were running pottery evening classes in the town. She had always fancied taking up a creative pastime but never quite got round to it. She had PM'd the girl to ask for details and very quickly got a return message saying that there had been a cancellation for the following evening's group in the church hall at 7pm. After messaging back and forth to confirm details, cost and the fact that novices were welcome, Amber had signed herself up.

Later that evening when Jamie joined her in bed, she had felt a little guilty for being such a moody cow and had responded to his unexpected advances, despite the fact that it was only Tuesday. As usual, she had ended up on top, jiggling her boobs in his face, although she had faked her orgasm to speed things up a bit as she was still a bit too wound up to come, and she couldn't be bothered with the energy it would take to keep her legs clenched, and fantasise about George Clooney turning up on her doorstep with a bunch of roses and a twinkle in his eye.

The following evening, she had left the house at 6.30pm leaving Jamie open-mouthed in the kitchen, as she explained to him that: yes, she was going out; no, she wouldn't be back all that late; and, yes, he would have to 'do his own dinner', which basically meant sticking the plate of dinner she had prepared for him into the microwave!

She had left the house feeling ridiculously liberated for someone who was only popping out to a local pottery class, but then it also made her realise how little she had done for herself lately. When the kids were at home it had been all about them, which she had loved, but now they were away, she pretty much existed as Jamie's beck-and-call girl. He wasn't mean to her or anything, and certainly didn't say she couldn't *do* stuff, but it had become easier and easier to just go along with his plans rather than risk the Spanish inquisition if she did decide to go out after tea time!

She was more than a little nervous as she pulled into the church carpark. She had deliberated for ages about what to wear. She hadn't wanted to look too smart, as if she was going for a job interview, nor had she wanted to look like she made a bit too much effort for a pottery class, so she'd gone for nonchalantly casual; as if she always wore Converse trainers with chinos and a scarf draped artily around her neck. She'd taken a bit of time to train her curls into a 'messy bun', which was actually a lot more work than a 'neat bun' could ever have been, and she had actually applied foundation, eyeliner, mascara AND eyebrow pencil – although she had taken care not to overdo the eyebrows like some of the young girls tended to do these days ending up looking like two giant slugs had fallen asleep above their eyes! She had applied lip plumping gloss which did indeed make her lips look slightly pouty as opposed to 'stung by a bee due to an addiction to fillers'!

Amber took a deep breath and made her way into the hall; she felt like the new kid in school. The room was already occupied by around 10 women of varying shapes and sizes – some quite frumpy, some more wacky with purple hair and facial piercings. Amber stood uncomfortably in the doorway, unsure about where to sit. There were a few trestle tables dotted around the room, each with a chair at either end. Some of the tables were already taken and Amber really didn't want to muscle-in on any of the ladies waiting for a friend. Mercifully, before she'd had time to dither much longer, and before she took root in the doorway, a friendly women of about her age came bounding up to her and took her by the hand, guiding her to one of the empty tables.

"Come and sit with me. I don't want to get lumbered with the frumpy ones," she said in a low voice.

Normally Amber would have shied away from such over-familiarity at a first meeting, but to be honest she was really glad that the decision of 'who to sit with', had been taken out of her hands.

She sat next to her new acquaintance who introduced herself as Freya. Freya was slim, flame-haired and impossibly bo-ho. She was friendly and down to earth and Amber warmed to her instantly. They chatted away comfortably – that is, Freya chatted while Amber interjected only when Freya paused for breath – and were giggling away like a couple of naughty school girls when 'HE' entered the room.

"Fucking hell," muttered Amber on an inward breath, "Who is that?"

"That my darling is Franc; with a 'c'."

Amber didn't think she had ever seen anyone quite so handsome as Franc with a 'c'. He was tall and slim, with broad muscular shoulders and dark, wavy hair that fell sexily across his forehead. He was dressed in faded Levis, a dark T-shirt and an apron tied around his waist. Who else could look that good in a bloody apron? He was also wearing flip-flops. Amber had long since harbored a fetish for bare-footed men especially when they had feet as beautiful as Franc; tanned like the rest of him, with long slender toes, and short clipped toenails. What was it about a bare-footed man that made him look so impossibly wild and free; manly, yet vulnerable at the same time? She remembered the hero in one of her books, who had whisked his girlfriend off to a paradise island, where they had spent their days barefoot in the sand, before making love to the sound of crashing waves in a candlelit bedroom with French doors that opened out onto their own private beach. She had tried to persuade Jamie to wear flip-flops for a while after that, but he had told her 'she had to be bloody joking if she thought he was going to prance around in a pair of bird's shoes'!

Franc certainly looked nothing like a 'bloke in a girl's shoes'; he was *all* man!

"Put your tongue back in, girl!" Freya had laughed.

Amber had blushed and bought herself back to reality. She was pretty sure she had been gawping, she only hoped she hadn't actually dribbled!

"Bit too pretty for my taste," smiled Freya, "but I get the appeal, and he's certainly got a marvelous backside!"

As Franc turned around, Amber noticed that he did indeed have a 'marvelous backside', and was little ashamed of how her lady parts were reacting to the delectable Franc!

The evening passed in a flurry of giggles and messy fun. Amber learned that Freya had been coming to Franc's pottery class for about a month and had been desperate for someone to join who wasn't a 'frumpy old bore'. She had also learned that Franc was short for Franco and this explained his olive tanned skin, jet black hair and general Italian gorgeous-ness. Franc was attentive, impossibly arty and according to Freya; giving Amber the 'once over'. Amber had giggled nervously, and profusely denied any possible interest from Franc, whilst noticing that Franc did seem to catch her eye every time she looked his way – which was admittedly fairly often - usually to listen to his instruction, but occasionally to ogle his bare feet and glorious backside!

After pottery class, she had blushed the colour of a boiled beetroot as Franc had kissed her on both cheeks as they thanked him for his class. (He *had* kissed each and every one of them on the cheeks, but she did think he had lingered a little longer with her than with frumpy Brenda on table four!)

They left the church hall laughing and chatting like they had known each other for years. They had even stopped for a very sophisticated glass of Prosecco in the posh wine bar opposite the church; much to the chagrin of Jamie when she had returned home a full hour later than planned! The hypocrisy of a man who was sniffy about her lateness when he regularly returned three hours later than planned without a moment's concern, whilst she tried desperately to keep his dinner warm, was not lost on her!

That night, she wasn't entirely convinced that she hadn't had an orgasm in her sleep, but she knew for sure that whatever had happened had been due to the outrageously filthy dream she'd had about Franc!

The week passed in a blur of mundanity; washing, cooking, shopping, ironing clothes that got chucked on the bedroom floor two hours after wearing them. Amber felt herself longing for Wednesday night. She was really looking forward to chatting with Freya again (and of course the chance to ogle Franc's marvelous backside) and escaping the humdrum of her life. It was like she was bloody invisible. She began to mentally take note of the conversations she and Jamie had and she reckoned that the requests for cups of tea, the time of the next meal, and the location of his sodding underwear even though it was housed in exactly the same location as it had always been, outweighed any idle or pleasant chit chat about 80:1. She began to feel increasingly like the hired help, although the hours were shit and the pay was even worse – as for job satisfaction or employee bonuses; forget it! She began to wonder if she and Jamie had anything in common anymore; or, worse, if indeed they ever had.

Wednesday night came around and Amber embraced it like a shore-hungry sailor. She couldn't ignore the butterflies in her tummy as she dressed in the pale pink chinos she had bought on sale in Primark and the new Converse pumps complete with pink sparkle detail and definitely NOT on sale! When Jamie had commented on her 'getting tarted-up in new clothes', she had simply told him that she'd had the trousers ages and that the pumps were a treat with her leftover birthday money. (This was almost true in that she *had* found a spare fiver tucked inside her phone case which was probably leftover from her birthday money – she hadn't told him that the other 60 quid had come from the food shopping money and was the sole reason they'd eaten budget sausages and jacket potatoes all week – he didn't need to know that!)

He'd sulked a bit when he realised that she was *actually* going out and not just 'teasing'. She'd marvelled at the arrogance of a man who wouldn't normally notice if she was lying dead on the kitchen floor, providing his tea had been cooked and there were no dirty pots in the sink, and who also thought she wouldn't *actually* dare to go out two weeks in a row! So far that week, he'd played pool on two nights (once in the tournament and once because he needed to 'practise his game' like he was Jimmy-fucking-White or something!), and a twilight game of golf with a 'prospective client', who Amber had known all along was his mate Ralph who he already did work for! On all three occasions Amber had faithfully kept his dinner warm, only to be told that it was a bit burnt/dried up, or that he'd already eaten! They'd had one conversation that she could remember about the kids, and the rest of the time she had read her book while he had flicked his way through the TV channels whilst farting on the couch next to her. They hadn't even had their Saturday night shag, although she had to confess that she'd deliberately stayed up late to watch 'Locked up – My Jail Hell', in the hope that he'd be asleep by the time she came to bed.

It was ironic, Amber thought, how much more notice he took of her when she wasn't around than when she was running around after him like a skivvy! She had ignored his stomping around the house, purposely banging cupboard doors in his search for stuff that was right under his bloody nose and applied a last splash of 'strawberry kiss' lip-gloss. She had picked up her bag and keys and left the house not bothering to say goodbye. He wouldn't have heard her anyway – he was too busy moaning about having, 'been at work all day and coming home to do his own fucking dinner'! Amber decided that if slaving over a homemade lasagne and leaving it on a plate for him to microwave was so unappreciated then next week she would just the leave the takeaway menu by the phone – fuck it! She was done with taking care of a six foot 3-year-old!

She drove the short journey to the church hall and parked in the car park. Her hands were ridiculously clammy as she grabbed her handbag from the foot well, and she was sure her heart didn't normally beat that fast! She checked her reflection one last time and tried to kid herself she was only checking that she didn't have lipstick on her teeth.

As she entered the church hall she scanned the room desperately for Freya; as much as she had been looking forward to perving over Franc, she wasn't yet confident enough to sit comfortably in a room full of strangers without an ally. Fortunately for Amber, she had heard Freya's voice before she saw her and she had breathed an inward sigh of relief. They sat at their usual table and listened intently to Franc's instructions on how to treat the clay as, 'an extension of your body'. Amber wasn't entirely certain what he had meant by this, but she had very much enjoyed watching him manipulate the soft clay and had rather naughtily imagined him doing the same to her breasts!

Freya had teased her for shamelessly ogling Franc with her mouth open and Amber had rather unsuccessfully tried to deny that she had been doing anything other than watching Franc's tuition. Once again, Amber's mind had begun to wander and she found herself imagining the beautiful Franc on top of her, running his tongue gently from the tips of her toes to the tender flesh on the inside of her thighs as she arched her back in anticipation, sultry eyes half-closed, lying on crisp white sheets, champagne in the ice bucket, soft music playing in the background…..she had a feeling she would need a whole bucket of ice to cool her down if she dreamed much longer - she was like a bloody bitch on heat!

The session ended all too soon and Amber found herself hoping that Franc would kiss her goodbye – if only briefly. He did not disappoint and she found herself breathing in the musky smell of his aftershave and revelling in the feel of his stubble brushing against her cheek. It was all she could do not to throw her arms around him and snog his face off whilst begging him to throw her over the work bench and bonk her brains out – although she didn't think frumpy Brenda would be all that impressed!

Amber and Freya had left the hall chatting and giggling like two hormonal school girls. They were just about to cross the road to the wine bar opposite when they heard a voice call out after them, "Ladies, your bag!"

Amber had turned around to see the delectable Franc running after them holding a bag which was obviously not theirs – partly because their bags were slung over their shoulders and partly because it was made of brown nylon and clearly the property of a forgetful octogenarian.

As he had neared them he had duly noted that they did indeed have their bags with them and had made an unconvincing apology for the inconvenience, after which he had proceeded to give them his card in case they 'needed any help', whilst never once breaking eye contact with Amber. Amber had felt the warmth rise up her neck and into her cheeks and had been pretty sure that she was now the colour of an over-ripe tomato. She would not have dared to tell anyone about the warm wet feeling in her nether regions!

"He was totally checking you out!" screamed Freya, none too quietly.

"Don't be daft," Amber had replied, "he just thought one of us had left our bag, that's all."

"Yeah, right!" said Freya. "I'm sure he genuinely

thought you or I would own a bag that looks like it belongs on SAGA shopping trip – and why would we 'need any help'? Although, judging by the colour of your face I can think of one or two things he might be able to 'help' you with!"

Freya had yelped in mock agony as Amber had punched her affectionately on the arm. They had continued on their way to the wine bar where they had indulged in a glass of fizz followed by a bit of impromptu karaoke. Amber couldn't remember when she had laughed so much and she wasn't sure if that made her happy or a little bit sad.

She had crept into the bedroom at a little after 11 that evening and climbed into bed next to Jamie.

"Where the fuck have you been?" he had growled, but Amber knew this was more about the indignation of having his sleep even slightly disturbed rather than a real concern as to where his wife had been. She could have been dead in a ditch for all he had cared just so long as she didn't wake him from his beauty sleep! She ignored his grumbling and snuggled down into the covers. If her dreams had been naughty last week, they were positively pornographic that night. Franc had whisked her away on a romantic boat trip (she had no idea where they had caught the boat considering they lived at least 60 miles from the coast) to a remote cottage where they had made love in front of a roaring fire and where Franc had sat close behind her at a potter's wheel teaching her to make pots from clay and running his wet and dirty hands all over her naked body, his erection pressed into her back – a kind of XXX rated version of the scene from Ghost where Patrick and Demi get it on over a bit of 'throwing'. The only thing spoiling Amber's fantasy was the fact that she couldn't touch herself while fantasising – she certainly didn't want her snoring, farting husband to think that her ardour was anything to do with him. She did consider going to sleep in the spare room or on the sofa but felt a bit guilty leaving him in bed to go and flick herself off over another man – whether he'd been an inconsiderate twat or not! Instead she had tossed and turned throughout her sleep, unbelievably frustrated and unable to properly relax.

Jamie had sulked with her for two full days after her 'night out'. To be honest, she hadn't actually minded that much. It had meant that she could be alone with her thoughts and that she hadn't had to make too much effort with the dinner. He'd eaten his on a tray on his lap in front of the TV while she had sat in the kitchen watching re-runs of Monarch of the Glen, which Jamie hated, and perusing Cosmopolitan for new ways to achieve 'smoky eyes'.

By the time Saturday had come around, and when he had realised that she wasn't going to fall on bended knee and beg for his forgiveness, Jamie had begun to attempt 'small talk' with Amber. He'd even offered to make her a coffee on Saturday morning and suggested they go out for a drink with their friends Adam and Davina that evening. To be truthful, Amber had never really liked Davina but had tolerated her for the sake of Adam and Jamie's friendship. Jamie and Adam had been friends since school and often played golf together. Adam was a lovely bloke, polite and easy-going but his wife was a high maintenance bitch in Amber's opinion. You never quite knew which Davina would come to the party – sometimes suspiciously pleasant, other times moody and temperamental. Davina was obsessed with image and was always bragging about her latest kitchen appliance or new soft furnishings. Amber herself wasn't adverse to the odd episode of 60 Minute Makeover, but there was only so long you could be interested in listening to someone wax lyrical about their new cushion covers and the advantages of ambient lighting! Davina's image obsession didn't stop at her house; it manifested itself in her personal appearance too. She was always coiffed to within an inch of her life, her nails were permanently manicured and, if it didn't have a designer label, then Davina didn't wear it. Amusingly, as she had begun to age, she had clearly developed an addiction to pumping her face full of all manner of toxic substances to ward off the effects of ageing. Initially this had had the effect of making her look pretty good for her age, but had increasingly begun to make her look permanently surprised and unable to show any kind of facial emotion. It was as though her face had been 'ironed' and her cheek bones and lips were definitely expanding at an alarming rate! The thing that pissed Amber off the most, was the pressure she felt to spend at least 3 fucking hours getting ready every time they went out with Adam and Davina. It was strange, really, because Amber genuinely had no desire to look like a cross between a Bratz doll and a puffer fish, yet she always felt strangely inadequate in Davina's company – mind you, that was probably a lot to do with the fact that Davina truly believed her own shit smelled of roses, rather than Amber's own personal short comings!

Amber had reluctantly agreed to going out and was pleased when Jamie offered her 20 quid to 'buy herself something nice'! Hardly the romantic gesture of the century, and more likely a sweetener so that he got his Saturday night shag, but Amber took it anyway. Unlike Davina she was a thrifty shopper and had become adept at teaming bargain bucket finds with a few accessories to look, if not a million dollars, then at least a few hundred!

Despite vowing not to pander to the social pressure of a night out with Davina, Amber found herself jumping into the shower a full three hours before they were due to go out and winding some twizzly curler things into her hair that promised to deliver 'natural ringlets without heat damage'. She had used the tutorial from Cosmopolitan to give herself truly smoky eyes (although she did have to have two tries, as the first attempt made her look like she'd gone 10 rounds with Frank Bruno) and had just about manged to pull off 'winged' eyeliner. She teamed the black jumpsuit she'd bought for under a tenner with some 'fuck me' heels, silver jewellery and a delicate black and silver choker. She had been quite pleased with the result and tried to stop thinking about whether Franc would fancy her looking like this.

As she came down the stairs, Jamie had barely looked up from his newspaper except to remind her that she'd taken bloody ages and he couldn't find his 'best watch'. Amber had sighed inwardly and resisted the urge to tell him 'find his own fucking watch'! She really believed that he wouldn't have noticed if she'd come downstairs stark-bollock naked, wearing nipple tassels and with a rose shoved up her bum. What did it matter if she fantasised about passionate sex with Franc? As long as she didn't block his view of the telly, Jamie wouldn't have noticed if Franc flipped her over the coffee table and shagged her senseless right in front of him!

They had gone to the local pub that night and Adam and Jamie had proceeded to spend the entire evening in the other bar playing pool. Davina was right on form has Adam had just bought her a convertible Mini Cooper for her birthday and had promised her a new conservatory and some Astro Turf. Amber was glad she didn't have any sharp implements about her person - she wasn't sure if she wanted to take her own life or Davina's! Amber resorted to drinking three large Proseccos and an Espresso Martini which went some way to easing the boredom of listening to Davina's superficial life story. At one point Amber became quite fixated upon Davina's frozen face and wondered what it felt like to have eyebrows that never moved.

"Amber, are you listening…?" Davina's voice snapped Amber from her thoughts and she returned to feigning interest in 'the world according to Davina'. She really did wonder how Adam put up with her.

When it was time to leave and Amber had pretended to be 'looking forward to going for dinner round at Adam and Davina's house' (she simply couldn't wait to see Davina's new glass coffee table), she was feeling pleasantly tipsy. She had responded to Jamie's drunken advances in the taxi home – it was ironic how he literally hadn't noticed her for the entire evening until he fancied a bit of nookie – and she had enjoyed their shag on the living room rug. They had burst in through the front door, shedding clothes as they went and practically fallen into the lounge. Jamie had struggled to find the zip to her jumpsuit (mainly because it didn't have one!) and Amber had resorted to removing her own clothes if they were ever going to get started. They had snogged passionately, if not a little sloppily, and all the while Amber had fantasised about the smell of Franc's aftershave and his soft stubble on her cheek. Jamie smelled more like lager and a late night kebab. Amber had practically come the moment Jamie put his head between her legs and she was fairly certain this was not simply due to Jamie's prowess at cunnilingus. She had resisted their usual, 'Amber on top position', and had instead gone onto all fours with her bottom seductively raised. This way she was able to imagine that it was Franc behind her, his strong hands holding onto her hips as he thrust deeply into her while she touched herself, feeling her own wetness. To her surprise (and definitely to Jamie's) she came again, something which had not happened in their *whole* relationship. Afterwards as she lay panting, she was surprised by her sexual awakening. Jamie rolled away from her, very un-seductively wiping himself on his discarded boxer shorts. "I've still got it babe," he slurred, before going to the loo to pee loudly for about 5 mins before bumping and swearing his way up the stairs.

Amber listened to the sound of Jamie's snoring coming from upstairs. She lay on the rug, in the dark, feeling guilty and ridiculously emotional. She padded into the kitchen and drunk a large glass of water before returning to the lounge to curl up under a blanket on the sofa. She couldn't face sleeping next to the man with whom she had spent her entire adult life, the man who had fathered her children, the man who had just had drunken sex with her on their living room floor and the man who she had wished was someone else the whole way through. She fought back the tears as she fell into a fitful sleep and wondered what the hell was going on with her.

Jamie had awoken like a bear with a sore head the next morning. He had always been a grumpy bugger with a hangover and this Sunday had been no exception. He had lounged around for the entire day whilst Amber had put the washing on, cooked Sunday dinner and cut the grass. He'd had a proper bitch fit because he'd stubbed his toe on the door frame while putting out the rubbish – which instantly became Amber's fault as this was the one job she'd asked him to do and therefore the reason he'd stubbed his bloody toe!

By the time evening had come Amber was glad to see the back of him as he heaved himself off the sofa leaving behind an impression like a body outline in a crime scene! He had mumbled something about 'feeling rough' and gone to bed. Amber had marvelled at how somehow who felt so 'rough' had still managed to drink about 10 cups of tea, eat an egg and bacon sandwich, a roast beef dinner with three Yorkshire puddings, an enormous portion of apple crumble and ice cream and a large family-sized bag of Twiglets!

Once he had gone, Amber stretched out on the sofa, turned off the TV (she wasn't really into watching some bloke with long hair and greasy hands turning a 1960's old banger into a 'retro classic'), and had settled down with her latest book – 'You will be mine'. She devoured page after page as the reluctant heroine was relentlessly pursued by the troubled billionaire out to prove his sincerity. He had finally worn her down with a trip to Rome – this being the birth place of her long lost father - and a hand-tied bunch of white orchids (her favourite flower of course!), delivered ceremoniously to her place of work. Amber herself would have settled for a night in a Premier Inn and a bunch of carnations from the Co-op right now, and from a man who actually noticed she was alive now and again! Was romance really only the stuff of fiction? Was she destined to spend the rest of her life disappointed and waiting for something that was really only the subject of fantasy?

When Amber had finally gone to bed it was well past midnight and she was knackered! She had to be in work at 9 on a Monday and she knew she would struggle to get up, let alone do her hair and make-up as her job required her to do. Not for the first time, she wished had the kind of job where she could just scrape her hair back and chuck on some leggings. Come to think of it, she wished she had any kind of job that was more rewarding than the make-up counter in Boots. She would have loved to do something creative – maybe she could be a potter's muse?! She certainly fancied the idea of spending the day getting dirty and creative with Franc!

Amber's week passed pretty much the same as any other – work, eat, housework, sleep, repeat. On more than one occasion she inwardly chastised herself for being ungrateful. She had a nice home, two lovely kids, a husband who loved her (well she presumed he did anyway) and food in her tummy. She had her health, all her own teeth – apart from the odd crown – and only a few grey hairs which she covered with highlights anyway. There were starving children in the world and here she was moaning about her misfortune and being dissatisfied with her lot in life.

She really tried hard to 'cheer up', however she was never as cheerful as when Wednesday came around again. Jamie had told her that he was going out to play pool with Rick as she was, 'off out gallivanting with her hippy friends again'. Amber hadn't bothered to react but had simply smiled and told him she thought that was a great idea!

"I might even go to a club after, so don't wait up!" had been Jamie's response.

Once again Amber had refused to rise to the obvious (and fairly childish) bait, and had not mentioned the unlikelihood of him finding a 'club' open on a Wednesday night.

"That's fine, love," she replied, and smiled to herself as he left, slamming the door and muttering something incoherent about, 'other men's fucking wives'!

Amber had arrived at the church hall and settled herself confidently at her's and Freya's usual table. How brazen she had become! Time was when she would have sat in a pub car park waiting patiently in the freezing cold for a friend rather than venture into an establishment on her own!

Freya had not yet arrived, and Amber was just about to text her when her phone beeped. *Sorry hun, at my mum's she had a fall. Didn't tell you earlier cos I knew you'd cancel without me! Have fun! F xxx*

'Oh fuck!' thought Amber. Freya was absolutely right – she would definitely *not* have come on her own. Bloody cowbag! Amber scrabbled around on the floor for her bag that she had just accidentally emptied in her fluster; if she sneaked out quietly now, no-one would notice she'd gone. There was no way she wanted to sit with frumpy Brenda and her floral-skirt-wearing friends, and she *definitely* couldn't stay on her own.

She was just about to stand up to make her exit, when she noticed a pair of tanned, flip-flop clad feet, just inches away from her as she knelt on the floor, scooping up a stray lip-gloss and a box of tic-tacs. She felt her heart beat wildly in her chest, and the colour begin to rise in her cheeks. The lip-gloss rolled further away from her as she fumbled around. She reached out her hand at the same time as strong, slender fingers curled themselves around both the lip-gloss and her own trembling fingers. This gesture had an alarming effect on Amber's lady parts and she wasn't entirely sure that she wasn't going to orgasm on the spot (that would have been a corker of an entry for Cosmopolitan's 'Top Ten Most Unusual Orgasms' – 'How I came over a lip-gloss at a pottery workshop in a church hall'!)

"Let me help you," Amber nervously raised her head at the sound of Franc's voice; her shaking, and now positively clammy, fingers still clutching the lip-gloss *and* Franc's hand.

"Oh, er, no…er, it's fine…I was, er…I was just leaving," Amber had stammered. Her knees were starting to stiffen from her awkward position crouching on the floor, and she felt suddenly light-headed.

"Leaving?" replied Franc. "Why are you leaving – you are my most promising student."

He had given her a wink then, as he spoke, and smiled wryly, his eyes boring into hers. Amber had tried to speak but only a squeak had escaped her lips. As she attempted to raise herself from the floor, she had almost lost her balance and Franc's strong arm had encircled her shoulders, helping her to her feet, his other hand still curled tightly around hers. Amber was unable to remove her gaze from his, despite the intensity.

"My, er, friend…she er…she can't make it," Amber managed to say, in a soft breathy voice that didn't quite sound like her own. Suddenly she had become aware that she was still holding Franc's hand and, embarrassed, she pulled her fingers from his grasp.

"Please stay," said Franc. "I will look after you, I promise," and once again gave her a wink and a smile that reduced her to jelly.

Amber sat back down in her seat, not because she wanted to stay (she still felt uncomfortable without Freya) but because she was sure that if she didn't sit down she would literally melt into a big, wet puddle on the floor! She had busied herself with pretending to look for something in her bag as she tried to compose her breathing and calm her pounding heart. As she lifted her eyes briefly, she once again caught Franc's eyes, gazing in her direction. Good grief, she was going to have a bloody coronary if this carried on!

As the session got under way, Amber became engrossed in her first attempt at sculpture which, mercifully, went some way to calming the nerves she felt whenever Franc came within a foot of her table, or when his hands 'accidentally' brushed hers as he advised her on her technique, or when she felt his warm breath on the back of her neck as he leaned in behind her. She was in serious need of a cold shower when she got in; that, and perhaps a quick session with the vibrator that she had won at a friend's Ann Summer's party and never used!

At the end of the class, Amber collected up her things and prepared to leave. Just as she made her way to the door she felt Franc's hand on her shoulder.

"Can I join you?" he asked, and then clarified as he noticed Amber's puzzled expression, "...For a drink. You and your friend always go for a drink afterwards, don't you?"

Amber was so taken aback by his direct approach, that she was lost for a reply. When she did try to move her mouth to speak, Franc pulled her in tighter towards him and whispered in her ear, "I'll just lock up and see you in the wine bar in 5 minutes – my treat."

Amber turned to protest but Franc had already walked away and left her dumbstruck, opening and closing her mouth like a bloody goldfish!

As she walked into the wine bar, Amber wondered what the hell she was doing there. Going to have drinks with a man who had practically made her come over a dropped lip-gloss, and waiting for him, alone, in a bar – something she had literally NEVER done in her entire life! She thought that maybe she was having a mid-life crisis; a bit like Shirley Valentine, except not on a Greek island – although Franc was certainly dark and exotic!

Amber found a table in the corner of the bar, away from the door. She didn't want to risk being spotted by anyone she knew, although none of her and Jamie's friends would be likely to be found in this part of town, and certainly *nowhere* near the church hall! She felt ridiculously on edge and sat precariously on her chair, fidgeting nervously with the magnetic catch on her phone case. As she heard the door, she knew instinctively that it was him. He sauntered casually over to her table.

"What can I get for you?" he asked in his soft voice, the traces of his Mediterranean accent still obvious to the ear.

"I didn't get a drink, because I didn't know what you like," faltered Amber.

"Don't be ridiculous, I wouldn't hear of a lady buying the drinks," he smiled, holding her gaze.

Amber blushed furiously and smiled back weakly. "I…er…I don't know, maybe I'll have…"

Franc interrupted before she had time to finish, "Will you allow me to surprise you Tresoro?"

Amber didn't have much of the Italian language under her belt but she assumed the 'Tresoro' had something to do with 'treasure' and was therefore a term of endearment. She blushed more furiously than before and felt that her cheeks were on fire. Unable to speak, she just nodded her head.

Franc returned with a luscious-looking red cocktail, served in a tall elegant glass with a frosted sugar rim and ripe, red cherries hanging over the edge.

"It's called a 'kiss on the lips'," said Franc, flashing her his most seductive smile.

If Amber's cheeks had been red before, they were now positively crimson and rivalled the colour of her bright red drink. She took the cocktail from Franc and sucked greedily on the straw – she'd never needed a drink so badly in all her life – her nerves were shot to bits!

Franc watched her intently as she sucked on the straw.

She had never been all that perceptive when it came to men's advances but even she could see the look of desire on his face. Besides, it was very difficult to suck on a straw, in the company of a smoking hot, and flirtatious, Italian without looking like a porn star!

She placed her drink back down on the table feeling a little light-headed from the sudden shot of alcohol. Franc continued to gaze at her.

"You are very beautiful," he commented seriously.

Amber attempted to shrug off his compliment but he placed his hand on hers, giving her a warning look.

"You must know how beautiful you are," he repeated, stroking the back of her hand with soft, soothing strokes.

Amber's insides had literally turned to jelly by now and she really did not know what to say. She gazed at his full lips and wondered what it would be like to feel them on hers. Suddenly a wave of guilt overcame her – what was she doing, sitting in a wine bar with a stranger (albeit a sex-on-legs stranger), gazing at his mouth with her tongue practically hanging out, longing for him to kiss her?

"I'm married," she had blurted out suddenly.

"I hope he knows how lucky he is," replied Franc softly.

Amber wasn't at all sure that Jamie had any idea how 'lucky' he was. She wasn't altogether certain he would remember who she was if he didn't run out of socks from time to time! She went back to sipping on her drink while Franc continued to watch her and make small talk.

He told her about growing up in Venice and she imagined him barefoot on the back of a gondola, his dark curls blowing in the breeze, his broad, tanned shoulders exposed in the sunlight. He asked her about her job and her life –but not about her marriage – and he chastised her when she was self-critical about how little she had achieved. He told her that she had real creative talent and, whilst Amber imagined that he said that to all the girls, he made her feel, in that moment, like she could achieve anything; that she had so much more locked up inside her.

She declined his offer of a second drink –she did have to drive, after all – and she really didn't trust herself not to drag him into the toilets and ravage him there and then with the bravado that too much alcohol would definitely create.

As they left the wine bar, Franc had held the door open for her, guiding her through it, his hand placed gently on her lower back. He had walked her to her car and waited patiently while she fumbled clumsily around in her bag, searching for her keys. Once she had opened the door with trembling fingers, he had turned her to face him and placed his hands on either side of her face. He had held her face and leaned in towards her, holding her gaze with an intensity the like of which she had never known. Then softly, ever so softly, he had placed his lips upon hers, caressing her gently with his mouth and touching her lips with the very tip of his tongue, before her own tongue found his; almost involuntarily. The kiss had lasted a mere few seconds, but Amber felt a throbbing in her loins and a beating in her chest that she could not quieten. He had pulled away from her and she had sat down in the driver seat of her car, wondering how she would ever be calm enough to drive the bloody thing home! He shut the door on her without speaking and raised his hand to his mouth as he blew her a kiss. Then he turned and walked away leaving Amber dumbfounded.

Amber drove home in a daze. She pulled her car into the drive, as if on auto-pilot, and walked up the path to her front door. She sighed inwardly as she considered the irony – here she was, walking up her front path, the path that had jokily been labelled as the 'path to Truelove', throughout her married life, and it she suddenly felt like the path to true love was definitely going in the opposite direction.

She turned her key in the front door and hung her keys and coat on the hook in the porch as she always did. She went through into the kitchen to make herself a coffee, with maybe a shot of brandy to calm her nerves, and flicked on the light.

At first she didn't notice Jamie sitting at the kitchen table, in the dark; it was only as she removed a cup from the cupboard that the sound of his voice behind her startled her enough to make her drop her cup.

"Jesus Christ! You scared me to bloody death. Why are you sitting in the dark?" she exclaimed.

"Waiting for my fucking wife to grace me with her presence," replied Jamie, in a dark tone that gave away its owner's less than sober demeanour.

"Oh for goodness sake, Jamie, I've been to a sodding pottery class," replied Amber sharply, her annoyance at his aggression quelling any guilt that she may have been feeling only seconds before.

Jami rose from the table on unsteady legs, "Been to the wine bar as well with your la-de-da friends …?"

He advanced towards her, clearly pissed off (not to mention pissed) at the cheek of her daring to have any kind of fun without him.

In that instant, Amber looked at the man she had spent her entire adult with, and wondered if she really knew him at all, let alone loved him. She wanted to tell him to 'fuck off and leave her alone', but, Amber being Amber, she attempted to pacify him and maintain the peace. She wondered to herself why she always felt the need to do that. Why she never quite mustered the strength to challenge him when he was belligerent or selfish?

"Yes, Jamie, I went for one drink then drove home," replied Amber, obviously neglecting to mention the knee-trembling kiss she had shared in the car park with her not so la-de-da 'friend'!

"No one else's fucking wife was in the wine bar," continued Jamie, still clearly not wanting to drop the subject.

"None of the wives of all of the men who were in the

pub?" replied Amber sarcastically, amazed at the hypocrisy of her husband's statement and her patience now wearing thin.

She continued to make herself a coffee, ignoring Jamie's jibes and grumbling. He continued to follow her around their not entirely cavernous kitchen, and his drunken rambling was seriously beginning to get on her increasingly frayed last nerve.

When she bumped into him for the third time as she attempted to empty the dishwasher in a bid to drown out his moaning about how he'd had to buy himself a bloody kebab for his tea, her temper snapped.

"Will you shut the fuck up?" she screamed, surprised at the forcefulness of her own voice. "I wash your shitty pants, cook your dinners, clean your house, tidy up the trail of fucking devastation that you leave behind you because you are too selfish to do it yourself and most mornings I also get the questionable pleasure of scraping your shit stains off the toilet. I *cannot* remember the last time you said thank you for anything, let alone bought me a bunch of fucking carnations from the garage, and the only time you have noticed me is when I have dared to venture out to a sodding pottery class at a church hall, and only then because it has fucked up any chance of you having your dinner on the table before you go to the pub which you have done, *every* week, whenever you fucking fancy! Now fuck off and leave me alone!"

Amber wasn't sure who was more surprised by her outburst – her or Jamie. He stood there, open-mouthed, as she threw her empty cup into the sink with such ferocity that it broke into several pieces. She then switched off the light and left him as she had found him, in the kitchen, in the dark.

She stomped up the stairs and into Holly's bedroom. She could not share a room with him tonight; she didn't trust herself not to put a pillow over his face while he slept. She crawled into Holly's bed and revelled in the comforting and familiar smell of her daughter. She cuddled up to one of the 'My Little Pony' teddies that her daughter had never managed to part with and considered the evening's events. She had felt such guilt at the kiss she had shared with Franc, but now she wasn't sure what she felt. She was somewhere between apathy and emotional exhaustion, if that was even possible. She had feared that she would not sleep a wink but, surprisingly, she fell asleep quickly and slept better than she had done in a long time. When she awoke, Jamie had already left for work and she was very grateful to have avoided any kind of confrontation – silent or otherwise.

She jumped into the shower and revelled in its invigorating heat. She washed and conditioned her hair, shaved her legs and even applied body moisturiser – something she hadn't bothered to do in far too long. She felt calm and detached inside. She dressed in her favourite skinny jeans and thin, dusky pink cashmere sweater. It was silent in the house and Amber had the strangest feeling – a sense of foreboding almost, like something life-changing was about to happen; something she couldn't quite put her finger on; until she went into the kitchen, which was…

On the kitchen table, in pride of place, were the broken pieces of the cup that she had thrown into the sink the night before and beside them, a note scrawled in pink highlighter (obviously the only pen he could find), "SORT YOUR FUCKING ATITUDE OUT!"

It was strange, in that instant, that the only thing she really noticed was the fact that Jamie had spelt attitude with only one 't', and it struck Amber as funny how such tiny insignificant details can often become so significant in potentially big situations. She cast her mind back to when her gran had died and, in her grief, Amber's mother had become obsessed with a packet of paper cake doilies that she had found stuffed in the back of a kitchen cupboard. It was as if that one tiny item had become representative of her gran's entire life, an item that her gran probably had long since forgotten, but an item that became of huge importance to her mother. She remembered they had argued over whether to throw the doilies away or keep them, and she thought her mother still had them to this day, now tinged yellow with age and far too creased as to be useable, tucked into the back of one of her own kitchen cupboards. It was as if focusing on the doilies was, for Amber's mum, a way to avoid dealing with the unbearable reality of having lost of her own mother. Amber was sure that, one day, she too would have her own 'doilies'.

Amber looked at the note and knew instinctively what she was going to do.

As she came back down the stairs, suitcase bumping down behind her, Amber took one last look at the home that she had once loved so much. She picked up the purple and white 'My Little Pony' from the hall table and tucked it under her arm as she heaved the case out to her car. She returned to the house just once more to visit the kitchen and place a small ^ in the relevant place in Jamie's use of the word ATITUDE, adding a small 't' to correct his spelling. And then, without a backward glance, she climbed into the car and drove away. It was then that she realised she didn't have a fucking clue where she was going!

Amber considered going to her mum's house but she really didn't want to worry her, especially as she had no real plan as yet. She also wasn't sure she even really wanted to talk about it – which was strange when you considered that she had potentially ended a 20-year marriage. She drove around for a while and thought about checking into a hotel but, although she had taken out a fair wad of cash from the cash point when she'd stopped to get petrol, it wouldn't be enough to last all that long and she wasn't convinced that Jamie wouldn't try to stop their credit card if he noticed her giving it a jolly good battering! Amber pulled into a layby and went to the snack wagon to buy herself a coffee. She sat in the car, sipping her coffee and pondering her next move.

At that moment her phone pinged and she found herself hoping that it wasn't Jamie. She had no desire to speak to him right now and she certainly was in no mood to explain herself – particularly as she wasn't sure that she even could right now! She glanced at the text and noticed it was from Freya.

Hi babe, you ok? Mum's fine, how was Franc?! F xx

Amber wondered how to reply. She wondered if she could talk to Freya about recent events. She didn't want her to feel obliged to help her; she barely knew her really, although Amber had to admit to herself that she felt closer to Freya in a couple of short meetings than she did with any of her current 'friends'.

Glad your mum's ok. I'm well tho I think I've just left my husband! A xx

Amber winced as she pressed the send button. Her phone rang almost before the message had a chance reach its destination.

"Oh my God, Amber, you ok?" gushed Freya's voice on the other end of the line.

"Yeah. I think so. Not sure how I feel, really," replied Amber.

"Where are you?" asked Freya.

"At the snack layby on the A219," replied Amber, suddenly aware of the madness of the morning's events.

"Come to me now," said Freya, "you can't sit there all day."

"I don't want to burden you with my shit," said Amber, "I wish I hadn't said anything, I'm ok really."

"Don't be bloody daft," said Freya. "Number 27, Hilltop Street, I'll put the kettle on."

"If you're sure …" said Amber, although deep down she felt grateful for the chance to at least collect her thoughts, and she wasn't sure the layby on the A219 was the best location for this.

"Shut up and get driving," said Freya, giving Amber the postcode to enter into her Sat Nav.

When Amber arrived at Freya's house, Freya had almost opened the door before Amber had got out of the car. She flung her arms around Amber's neck and hugged her tightly, kissing the side of her head.

"Come in, sweetie," said Freya, "I didn't bother with the coffee; I've poured us both a nice stiff gin and tonic!"

"Bloody hell, it's only 11 o'clock in the morning," laughed Amber.

"It's six o'clock somewhere in the world, sweetie," giggled Freya in reply.

Amber sat gratefully at the breakfast bar in Freya's small but gorgeously bo-ho kitchen. Freya's house was just like Freya – quirky and full of colour. Brightly coloured mugs and hand-painted china adorned a shabby yet stylish dresser in the kitchen. The house was a former worker's cottage, in which the downstairs rooms had all been knocked through to create an open-plan living space. On the other side of the kitchen area, Amber could see a plump, cushioned sofa, draped with soft, blankets in reds and golds. Mismatched chairs sat in the bay window and book cases fitted neatly into the recesses on either side of the open fireplace. A blanket box doubled as a coffee table, upon which sat a variety of candles in mosaic, jewelled, and coloured votives. The house was warm and inviting, neat yet busy with lots of beautiful knick-knacks, and impossibly stylish.

Amber felt instantly relaxed and almost like she had come home. She sat at the breakfast bar, trying to piece together the events of the last couple of days, and indeed the events of the last goodness knows how many years which had led up to this point. Freya listened quietly and basically just poured the gin.

Three large gins later, Amber was feeling quite pissed and a little emotional. When she began to cry, Freya took her by the hand and said,

"Come on, I'll show you where your room is."

"What do you mean, *my* room?" asked Amber.

"Well, you certainly can't go home right now and I'm guessing you're not up for going to your mum's?" asked Freya intuitively.

"Look, I'm sorry," said Amber, "I really didn't come here with that in mind. I don't think I had anything in mind really, but I certainly don't want to put you out."

"Look," said Freya, "it's just me and Dave here and we really love a visitor, don't we darling?" Freya smiled in the direction of a huge grey tabby cat with a black patch over one eye, as he forced his ample frame through the cat flap in the back door. At the mention of his name, he rubbed himself against Freya's legs purring loudly.

Amber smiled at the huge ball of fluff, twirling himself affectionately around Freya's ankles.

"Come on," said Freya, "I insist…unless you really don't want to?"

"I'd love to," said Amber, wiping her nose noisily and rather uncouthly on the sleeve of her cashmere sweater.

"Good, that's settled," said Freya. "Let's get your cases in and then you can have a nice hot, bubbly bath while I make us some lunch to soak up the gin!"

An hour later, Amber was sitting on Freya's sofa slurping noisily from a steaming hot bowl of homemade chicken stew. Her cases had been stored in the neat little spare bedroom with its iron-framed bed, crisp white sheets and turquoise and cerise pink cushions and throws. Amber would not have dreamed of putting those two colours together but the effect was beautiful. She had relaxed in the deep, hot bubbles in the claw-footed bath and, at Freya's insistence, had succumbed to an impossibly soft dressing gown in favour of getting dressed. Freya had said that there was no better time than today to enjoy a 'duvet day,' and you couldn't veg out properly in skinny jeans!

Despite having slept well last night, Amber felt suddenly shattered and was grateful for the haven that Freya had so kindly offered. They chatted most of the afternoon whilst watching a selection of girlie movies which they only half paid attention to. Amber learned that Freya had her own business, making jewellery, and also ran a couple of evening classes at the local college. Amber envied Freya's courage to do something that she enjoyed and was a little jealous; if only because she felt that she should have been braver in her own life.

It was only a little after seven in the evening when Amber found herself struggling to keep her eyes open. Dave was curled up on the sofa between them, snoring like an old train, and Amber was impossibly warm and cosy. She felt a little embarrassed by her uncontrollable 'head nodding', and hoped she hadn't inadvertently dribbled whilst sleeping!

"Come on, you; bed," said Freya, herding her up the stairs like an old mother hen.

"I'm sorry," said Amber, "must have been the lunchtime gin."

"Yeah, that and a tiny bit of emotional trauma," laughed Freya.

Amber smiled, inwardly noting that she'd had not one single call or text from Jamie. She wasn't sure if she felt relieved or upset. She wasn't convinced that she had anything to say to him but she also wasn't blind to the fact that he actually clearly didn't give much of a shit about where she was, or indeed if she was ok.

Amber climbed the stairs wearily and, after brushing her teeth, climbed into bed, not bothering to remove the warm dressing gown that she had 'vegged' in all afternoon. Her sleep was fitful – alternately deep and filled with weird dreams, followed by dozing and fidgeting. She awoke to find a text on her phone that had been sent at around 2.40am – *Thanks for letting me know you aren't dead!*

Amber assumed that Jamie had indulged in a couple of pints after work and had fully expected her to return home after her little 'tantrum'. She noticed he hadn't exactly been beside himself with worry but then she imagined that was a lot to with male bravado and not wanting to be the first to speak. God forbid he should actually have any questions about his own part in this mess!

Amber felt a pang of guilt at not letting him know she was ok – she guessed that was a little selfish. She typed out a quick reply, "I'm not dead."

Her phone pinged immediately, "You are taking the piss, where r u?"

She replied, "Just staying with Freya for a while, need some time."

Amber only half read his reply, which said something about 'fucking hippies' and him not being able to find his clean work trousers. She didn't bother to respond.

As she sat in Freya's kitchen sipping on the lovely hot latte that Freya had made using her state-of-the-art coffee machine, Amber wondered what the fuck had happened to her life. She really didn't have a clue about what to do next and she wasn't altogether sure how to feel about it all either. She chatted with Freya about the way things had become between her and Jamie, and found herself telling her new friend things that she didn't even realise she felt. She told her about her feelings of 'invisibility' in her married life, especially since her children had left home; she told her how unfulfilled she felt in her work life and about her dreams of a more creative career; and she told her that she didn't really feel that she had *any* true friends of her own – it was really surprising to Amber how little she knew about herself, or how much she had suppressed her own happiness and dreams in favour of looking after her family. Amber felt like Julia Roberts in that film where she plays a runaway bride, desperately searching for true love but never managing to quite be herself – morphing into her new husband to be, liking what he liked, going where he went. The film culminates with Julia's character trying several different types of eggs to discover the ones that she *actually* liked rather than only eating the eggs preferred by her most recent boyfriend. She ultimately decides that after years of eating eggs Benedict, she doesn't actually like them at all and much prefers eggs over easy – Amber had decided that maybe it was time she tried a few eggs of her own!

The rest of the day, and indeed the week, passed in a blur of window shopping, film watching and far too many late night 'heart to hearts' over several very large gin and tonics and more than one bottle of Prosecco. Amber wondered how her liver would cope with this sudden alcohol invasion. The two women laughed together, cried together, discussed romance, blow jobs and the dilemma of wanting to blow off during sex! Freya had explained about the last man she'd had a long term relationship with, who had basically run off with her so-called best friend, not to mention her life savings and a 'maxed-out' credit card. Freya admitted that she had done a shitload of crying, screaming and breaking lots of china, together with numerous trips to the bank to try and secure some kind of long-term payment plan to clear his debts and avoid losing her house in the process. Three years on she was totally over the bastard, although she couldn't deny still hoping that karma would come around the corner and throttle his cheating, thieving neck! She was solvent again, although considerably poorer than she had been, and was pretty content with her lot. She had a job that she loved, was answerable to nobody, and had become pretty good at finding things to do that didn't cost loads of money (hence joining the pottery class). She had also realised that you needed a surprisingly small amount of money to survive on, if you cleaned out the inconsequential crap from your life.

Amber had listened intently and really identified with what Freya was saying – it was time to take control - she wasn't quite ready to burn her bra and chain herself to the railings outside the council offices anytime soon – but she was definitely ready for some change! Amber had also realised her own part in the decline of her marriage. If she never spoke up, if she always took the path of least resistance, was always willing to 'do as expected' in order to maintain a quiet life, then she couldn't really blame others for taking the piss out of her good nature!

Jamie hadn't texted since the other morning and Amber really wasn't ready to speak to him yet either. She had felt ridiculously guilty when she had spoken to her children on the phone, as she did every week, but she reckoned they didn't need to know anything yet – besides which there wasn't really all that much to tell. The conversation with her son Dan had gone pretty much as it always did; a few brief pleasantries in his usual laid-back tone, before he told her he loved her and hung up, presumably to go back to having the wonderful carefree time that only the young can enjoy. Her daughter, Holly, had chatted merrily about this and that; new friends, new shoes which had meant she'd had to eat noodles for a week, who was snogging who; blissfully unaware that her parents should have any drama of their own. Amber was at least grateful that between them, she and Jamie had managed to raise two perfectly normal, happy kids who were now enjoying life to the full.

It hadn't escaped Amber's notice that Wednesday had come back around and that meant it was time for the weekly pottery class. She was still reeling from Franc's kiss last week and she hadn't quite had the nerve to tell Freya about it. She assumed he would have forgotten all about it by now anyway. She hadn't thought about him as much as she might have done, had it not been for the recent chaos in her life. The truth was, she didn't really feel all that guilty, and that made her feel guilty in itself. She decided not to mention pottery class and just wait to see if Freya was up for it. Sure enough when Amber got in from work that evening, Freya was dressed and applying a last flick of gloss in front of the hall mirror.

"Come on then my lovely, get your slap on, Franc won't fancy you in your lilac tabard," Freya had laughed as Amber came in through the door.

Amber had blushed and mumbled something about 'being ridiculous', but she couldn't deny the little flutter that occurred in heart, not to mention her lady bits, at the mention of his name!

Twenty minutes later, Amber had washed, piled her hair into a messy bun and refreshed her make-up (the one perk about working on a make-up counter was the opportunity to get made up in your afternoon break ready for a night out!).

The two women had resolved to grab a bite to eat in the tapas bar in town before their class and had therefore left early. Amber was really enjoying the freedom of coming in from work and dashing straight out again, not having to cook and only really having to worry about her own pants being washed! She felt 21 again and ridiculously wanton!

They had arrived at the church hall and settled at their usual table. Franc's appearance did not disappoint and Amber felt herself turn the colour of an over-boiled beetroot when he had looked her way. His smile and wink told her that he had definitely not forgotten about their kiss last week and she lowered her eyes in embarrassment.

"Fucking hell!" exclaimed Freya, a little too loudly (especially for frumpy Brenda's delicate ears).

"Ssssh!" said Amber, "we're getting daggers from Brenda."

"I'm not worried about Brenda," giggled Freya. "What the bloody hell went on with you two last week?"

"What do you mean?" squeaked Amber, her voice rising several octaves.

"You know *exactly* what I mean," Freya reprimanded. "If your face gets any redder you'll explode, and the way he looked at you was practically pornographic!"

"Nothing happened," replied Amber, squirming in her seat. "We went for a drink that's all…well ok, we may have kissed… but that's it, I swear, it was nothing…really!"

"That wasn't 'nothing' my darling," laughed Freya, "*that*

was foreplay!"

Amber could barely concentrate on her clay pot, and her trembling hands were proving pretty useless. Each time Franc came to their table (and that was often!) she got a feeling in her belly like she was descending in a high-speed lift. Freya had giggled and teased her mercilessly and Amber's nerves were in tatters by the time the class had ended. At the end of the session, just as they were leaving, Franc had kissed them goodbye, as indeed he did everyone, but Amber was fairly sure he hadn't flicked the merest hint of tongue across their earlobe as he had brushed their cheeks. She was also pretty sure that frumpy Brenda would have had a bloody coronary if he had done – although she wasn't certain sure her own heart was faring too well!

Freya had definitely spotted the extra attention that Franc had paid to Amber's unsuspecting left ear lobe and had given Amber a grin that would have rivalled that of a Cheshire cat on steroids.

"Are we drinking tonight, ladies?" Franc had enquired. It was seemingly an innocent question but Amber wasn't naïve enough not to realise that it was Franc's intention to join them.

"Of course," replied Freya, before Amber had a chance to speak (she wasn't altogether sure she had the power of speech anymore anyway!)

"See you there!" said Freya, winking at Amber.

Franc did not reply, but instead had looked directly at Amber and literally licked his lips, in a subtle but impossibly sexy fashion! Amber had nigh on melted into a puddle on the floor. When Franc had turned away, she had jabbed Freya in the ribs and told her to stop encouraging him.

"Oh, I don't think he needs much encouragement, sweetie!" laughed Freya.

They crossed the road to the wine bar, Amber on distinctly jelly legs, and took a table in the corner. Franc had joined them minutes later.

They had a surprisingly good laugh together. Franc just happened to have a fairly naughty sense of humour, and Freya and he acted as a catalyst for each other's jokes. Amber could not remember having such a laugh in ages. There were more than a few occasions in which Franc's hand 'accidentally' touched her knee and one where he shamelessly caressed a path from her knee to her thigh, brushing against her throbbing sex with the lightest of caresses. At this point, Amber had choked on her drink, practically spitting out her entire mouthful of Prosecco onto the table. This had somewhat killed the moment as Freya and Franc frantically tried to mop up her spilled drink and pat her on the back to prevent her from choking to death. If Amber had felt embarrassed at her less-than-cool reaction to Franc's touch, one look at his satisfied face told her that he was mighty pleased by her reaction; knowing full well the impact of his hands on her body.

Amber had excused herself and made her way to the ladies' toilet, needing some time alone to settle her nerves. This simply could not carry on. She had practically orgasmed in a crowded wine bar with her friend sitting right beside her – she was pretty sure that was sexually deviant in some eyes!

Amber walked down the long dark corridor to the loos, wondering why these swanky places seemed to always place the bathrooms so bloody far away. She entered the single toilet cubicle and locked the door behind her, grateful for the privacy. She held onto the basin with trembling hands and studied herself in the mirror. Her cheeks were flushed and her pupils wide. She splashed a little cool water onto her face, took a few deep breaths and steadied herself – mentally and physically. She slid the bolt across the door, preparing to leave and re-join her friends. She had only opened the door a fraction when she felt it being pulled from her grasp. In seconds, the door had opened and re-closed, leaving Amber still inside the toilet cubicle, taking a few seconds to realise what had happened. It didn't take long before she found herself looking into Franc's face. He had his back to the door, his hand still on the bolt that he had once again slid shut. His nose was millimetres from hers and his other hand had somehow snaked itself around her waist, drawing her in towards him. She could feel his warm breath on her face as he bent his head down towards her. Her breathing was shallow and she felt herself lean in closer to him. Her lips seem to part of their own accord and she could not take her eyes from his as they bore into her. He smelled of aftershave and soap and his body felt warm and hard against hers. He did not speak but lowered his lips to hers. His soft plump lips pressed tenderly against hers, she felt the flick of his tongue as he parted them and licked gently around the insides before finding her own willing tongue. Their tongues licked and flicked, softly and tentatively at first, before growing in intensity. Amber felt his passion as he claimed her, probing, as if trying to climb right inside her. She responded with a passion that she didn't know she possessed, surrendering completely to him. His hand, firmly on her lower back, pulled her closer into him as he took her with his mouth, his other hand moving to cup her face, his fingers entwined in her hair at the nape of her neck.

Amber felt her breathing become heavier and she began to pant, a small moan escaped her lips and she literally felt her legs buckle beneath her. Franc's strong arm caught her as she began to crumble and he pulled her tighter into him, so tight that she could feel his erection pressing against her.

He pulled her face away from his, pulling her back gently by her hair, his fingers still entwined. He moved away just far enough so that he could stare deep into her eyes. The intensity almost caused Amber to look away, but somehow she couldn't.

"I will make love to you, Tresoro," Amber heard

Franc's voice, as if in the distance.

She tried to compose herself, feeling bereft at the loss of his mouth on hers. Her lips were still parted, her breathing still heavy and she could feel the wetness in her knickers. Every part of her was throbbing, yearning for his touch.

"….but not here, in the bathroom," Franc's voice drifted back into her consciousness. He smiled at her, winked, and kissed her gently on the nose, before backing discreetly out of the bathroom.

Amber was unsure how long they had been in there – it could have been seconds, minutes or hours. All she did know was that she felt a longing like never before, the sexual chemistry between them was electric and she felt reckless and lustful!

Once again, Amber attempted to compose herself as she had done when she first entered the toilet – only then it was because of a little tickle on the leg – recovering from the oral onslaught that had been Franc's kiss was going to be a whole lot trickier. All the lustful romance she had read; never had she expected it to feel this good.

Amber made her way back to the bar where Franc and Freya were chatting innocently. He smiled at her as she sat down, but gave nothing away.

The evening ended far too soon and as they left the wine bar Franc had whispered in her ear as he gave her a chaste kiss on the cheek, "Tomorrow, Tresoro."

Amber didn't know what was happening tomorrow, but she had a feeling that Franc had a plan for her.

On the journey home, the two friends chatted about the evening and Amber confessed about Franc's brazen advances.

"Well, duh?!" exclaimed Freya. "I'm not blind you know, and I'm fully aware of how long it takes to have a quick pee. I also know that you don't come back from the toilet looking like you did unless you've been practically shagged in there!"

"I wasn't shagged," protested Amber, "it was just a kiss!" Although, deep down, she knew it was anything but, *just* a kiss.

Amber's dreams were vivid that night. She was unbelievably horny but was really not about to succumb to flicking herself off in her friend's spare bed like some desperate teenager! When she awoke, she was so wired and frustrated, she almost feared for the postman's safety if he lingered too long on the doorstep! She ate breakfast and rushed around; washing up, making beds, tidying, anything to keep her occupied – she just couldn't settle. Freya teased her and suggested she have a few minutes of 'alone time,' with her Tom Hardy calendar! Amber tried unsuccessfully to pretend that she was simply energised by a good night's sleep.

On the way to work that morning, realising the enormity of the lust she felt for Franc and the impending inevitability of them consummating that lust, she began to feel an overwhelming sense of guilt. What the fuck was she thinking? She was a married woman for goodness sake, albeit estranged at present, but her side of the marital bed was barely cold in the home she had shared with her husband for the last twenty years. What did she think she was doing, practically fucking a complete stranger in a wine bar toilet – what a classy bird she was! She wasn't exactly hopeful for her marriage to Jamie, he had been nonchalant about her departure to say the least, but he was still her husband and she at least owed him the courtesy of ending it properly before jumping into bed with her pottery teacher – whether he was sex on legs or not!

As she arrived at work, Amber had made three decisions: 1, she was going to speak to Jamie about their marriage; 2, she was going to ignore Franc's calls (even though she hadn't actually given him her number) until she was free to fuck his brains out guilt free; and 3, she was going to sort her life out regarding her job and personal fulfilment – quite a lot for a Thursday morning!

She busied herself on the make-up counter, displaying new products on auto-pilot, mentally chastising herself every time she thought of Franc's tongue deep in her mouth. She figured even if she did work things out with Jamie, it wasn't cheating if she just thought about it, right?! She'd done it enough bloody times over the years with more than one troubled billionaire – fantasised that was!

Amber reached under the counter to retrieve the revolting lilac tabard, resolving never to wear lilac again for as long as she lived, once she was her own boss. Just as she stood up from her crouched position, she noticed the rear profile of someone she recognised. It took her a few seconds to register the *very* familiar outline figure, dressed in trousers and a shirt that she was fairly sure she had ironed the week before. The figure that was behaving in an overly familiar fashion with his female companion, his arm draped loosely around her shoulders as they chatted next to a mannequin wearing a cable knit, fisherman's jumper. The very same figure that wouldn't have been seen dead in a cable knit jumper in the 20 years she had known him!

Jamie turned his head briefly to look her way, barely acknowledging her, except for the hint of a smug grin on his face. He turned back to his companion, laughing in a grossly over-exaggerated manner at her apparent witticism.

Fucking wanker!

Amber seethed inside; here she was agonising over the state of her marriage (well maybe not exactly agonising, but certainly feeling conscientious enough to at least give the tiniest bit of a shit!) and here *he* was, parading his new floozy in front of her. She wasn't stupid enough not to realise that the encounter was entirely deliberate on Jamie's part – it wasn't exactly like he hadn't realised she would be working on the make-up counter of this department store where she had worked for the last 20 fucking years! What the hell did he think he was playing at? Was he *really* having an affair or simply trying to make her realise what she was missing? Either way, he was being an arrogant twat, and this recent bout of what could only be described as 15-year-old behaviour had only served to make Amber realise *exactly* what she was missing – and unfortunately for Jamie, it wasn't him!

It was in that moment that Amber revised her three earlier decisions: 1, She was *not* going to speak to Jamie about the state of her marriage; 2, she was going to give Franc her phone number so that he *could* bloody well call her; and 3, she was absolutely, definitely, 100% going to sort her life out regarding her job and personal fulfilment!

When she left work that day, Amber felt a resolve and determination inside her that almost scared her – the worm had not only turned, she had rolled up her sleeves, donned her hobnail boots and was hell-bent on kicking the arse of anyone who dared to stand in her way!

She had popped into her local careers advice bureau on the way home (although, to be fair, they had been about as much use as a chocolate teapot, having very little idea about what she could do next other than working in a different retail sector – not exactly the groundbreaking adventure she was after!). She had also made an appointment with her local bank for the following week to discuss small business loans. Amber had the seed of an idea growing within her, and seeing Freya's collection of beautiful handmade jewellery and only served to fuel that idea.

About a five minute drive from Freya's house, Amber had swung into the carpark of the local grocery store to pick up a bottle of Prosecco – she had an overwhelming urge to celebrate, albeit the unknown – and heard her phone ringing from inside her bag. She hadn't checked her phone all day, her mind had been so busy, and she was surprised to see four missed calls. She didn't recognise the number and answered tentatively, convinced it was probably someone in Manchester offering compensation for her recent 'accident'.

"Hello?" she said.

"Tresoro. Where are you?" the deep familiar tones of Franc caressed her ears.

"Hello? Franc?" she answered, bewildered. "You've got my number!" Inwardly Amber chastised herself for stating the bleeding obvious and sounding so ridiculously uncool.

"Of course," replied Franc, "I had your number from the day you came into my life."

Amber was bloody glad she was sitting down, or she might have dissolved into a puddle on the floor – seriously, this man had the ability to reduce her to jelly with just a few words. Amber tried mentally to compose herself as her mind wandered to the very delicious mouth from which those words had come.

"Oh," was the only answer she could manage!

"Shall I pick you up?" said Franc, breaking Amber's thoughts.

"Pick me up?" asked Amber.

"Tonight?" replied Amber.

"Of course, Tresoro. Tonight."

Amber cast her mind back to the words that Franc had whispered in her eye the evening before. Her tummy took an involuntary lurch, and she wasn't sure *what* was happening in her nether regions!

"Well, I don't know… I mean… er…," Amber stuttered, as she tried to find her voice. There was a part of her that wanted nothing more than to leap into bed with Franc, but then the voice of reason was there to remind her that she barely knew him; he could be an Italian axe murderer for all she knew! She didn't even dare think about the fact that she hadn't slept with anyone other than Jamie in the last 20 years and she wasn't altogether sure how she felt about exposing her wobbly bits to a total stranger – especially a demi-God stranger like Franc.

"We can take it slowly," said Franc. "Maybe just a drink, I don't want to make you uncomfortable."

"It's been a long time," said Amber quietly.

"I can wait a little longer then," replied Franc gently. "I

will meet you in the wine bar and you can decide how you feel. It's all about you, Tresoro."

Amber quite liked the idea of it being 'all about her', for once. She shoved the voice of reason back into its self-righteous box and thought 'fuck it!' why not?

"7.30," she said, with a courage she did not exactly feel!

She returned home to Freya's – it was funny how it felt so much like home so quickly – and relayed the details of her phone call with Franc. She was so nervous at the prospect of meeting up with him, that she almost forgot to tell about her encounter with Jamie in the store that morning.

"What a twat!" declared Freya. "Good for you, bit of fun will do you good. Just be careful, don't put yourself into any compromising positions – unless you want to of course!"

"Not quite sure I trust myself to be in any kind of positions with Franc – compromising or not," laughed Amber.

Amber agreed that she would keep Freya on speed dial and keep her informed of the evening's events – if indeed there were any. They agreed a special signal if she felt in danger and Freya put a track on Amber's phone – just in case. Deep down, for some reason, Amber did not feel that she was in danger from Franc – he was well known in the community and could easily be tracked through the pottery class – unless of course you counted orgasmic fallout!

She dressed in a soft jersey, wrap-around dress in pale pink that fitted snugly around her waist, flaring out at her hips and barely skimming her knees. She added a subtle pink velvet choker, and twisted her hair into a low chignon, allow wispy tendrils to escape, framing her face. She applied natural make up, paying particular attention to accentuating her lashes and applying a pale pink gloss that made her lips look full and shiny.

She parked in the church car park, opposite the wine

bar, at 7.35pm. She did not want to appear too keen, nor did she want to be sitting in the wine bar alone, waiting for Franc to arrive – besides, if she was a little late she would know instantly if he had decided to stand her up, she reasoned.

As soon as she entered the wine bar, she could almost feel his presence before she saw him. He stood up from his seat in the corner and walked towards her, placing a soft, warm kiss full on her lips. He lingered for such a time that it was almost indecent, unhindered as he was this time by the constraints of other guests. Amber felt her heart beat quicken and her breathing becoming shallow as seemed to happen every time Franc was within one foot of her – let alone with his lips placed on hers.

"Come," said Franc, taking her by the hand and leading over to the table he had chosen. "Another kiss on the lips," he smiled, motioning to the cocktail on the table in front of her. "It seemed fitting – I hope it's the second of many more." The wink he gave as he said this should clearly have come with a government health warning, Amber thought to herself, and she sipped greedily at the drink, trying desperately to steady her nerves.

This time, there was no observing of personal space from Franc. With no other guests at their table, and a kiss in their shared history that would have rivalled any shag fest, he sat as close to Amber as possibly could without actually pulling her into his lap. His hand never left her upper thigh as he spoke and his eyes undressed her as he spoke. Now and again his thumb would skim the apex between her thighs, brushing delicately across her clitoris which by now was pulsating and thrusting itself shamelessly in his direction. Amber literally had no control over her wanton lady parts and she marvelled at the way her body had recklessly abandoned any connection with her brain and its diminishing ability to deliver coherent thought.

They laughed and they talked and, now and again,

Franc would lean in to her, even closer, grazing her neck with those deliciously soft lips of his, upon which her nipples would jump to attention like a soldier on parade. On more than one occasion, Amber completely lost the thread of her conversation as she imagined those lips on her erect nipples; sucking them into the warm wetness of his mouth, teasing them with his teeth whilst his thumb continued to graze her swollen clit. She wasn't entirely sure how much more she could take; if she thought her erotic fiction had got her in the mood, she clearly hadn't considered the 'Franc effect.'

"I think we should go," said Franc, as he nibbled her ear lobe.

"Go?" said Amber.

"To bed," said Franc.

Fucking hell! Amber almost orgasmed on the spot, she was literally lost for words. "I, er… I…"

"Don't be afraid, Tresoro," said Franc, continuing his sweet, torturous assault on her right ear lobe. "Remember, it's all just for you – nice and slowly. Not too much."

Amber wasn't entirely sure what constituted 'too much', but she did know that if she stayed in this wine bar a moment longer with him rubbing her lady garden and tongue-fucking her ears, she was going to have a 'Meg Ryan' moment and start banging her hands on the table and screaming, 'Yes, Yes, YES!' – although she certainly wouldn't be faking it!

Franc stood and took her masterfully by the hand, although Amber did notice that he took a moment to 'rearrange' himself before standing! He guided her gently through the door with his hand on her lower back – Amber had long dreamt of a man guiding her in this way, she had always thought it impossibly sexy and gently dominant.

They left the wine bar, and Amber realised she didn't even know where they were going. Seeming to sense her question, Franc said,

"To my place – it's very close."

He led round to the back of the church hall and down a small foot path that led to a little group of buildings which were barely more than cabins. There were about 3 or 4 cabins tucked away in a small, secluded garden and Amber once again felt a little uneasy as the voice of reason warned about the dangers of coming to a secluded cabin, down an unlit footpath, with a man whose sole intention was to ravish you but 'not too much'!

"I have to phone my friend," said Amber quietly.

"Of course, Tresoro," said Franc, "I understand. I promise I will take very good care of you."

That's exactly what I am worried about, thought Amber!

Franc opened the door to the cabin, explaining that the buildings were owned by the church and rented out to local artists and authors as part of an incentive to bring creative talent to the town. The interior was simple yet stylish, as only an artist's home could be. The living area was completely open-plan with a small sofa in front of a wood burner, at one end and a kitchen area at the other. One wall was covered entirely in free standing shelving upon which sat a plethora of some truly beautiful pots, vases and dishes in an array of bright coloured glazes. Objects of every size shape and design, some long and slender, others round and full with fluted openings. Amber had not seen anything so beautiful in a long time and she marvelled at the creativity behind the creation of this amazing pottery. Two doors led off the main living area and Amber's heart skipped a beat when she realised that one of these doors probably led to Franc's bedroom.

Franc motioned for her to sit at the small kitchen table while he began to pour them a glass of wine in two elegant goblets. He encouraged her to phone Freya, whilst he sat at the table beside her, watching her intently as she spoke. When Freya asked to speak to him, he took the phone from Amber's hand, his eyes never leaving Amber and a wry smile on his face as he spoke.

"You have my word, I will take *very* good care of her; she will be home by midnight."

Amber tried hard to ignore the tiny part of her (mainly the part located in her underwear) that had hoped she might be staying the night. What the heck was happening to her? She was behaving like a sex-starved lunatic!

When Franc had hung up on Freya, he took Amber by the hand and led her towards one of the doors that Amber had noticed upon her arrival. Sure enough, as he led her through, it did indeed turn out to be his bedroom. There was small armoire in the corner and a large bed dominated the centre of the small room. Surprisingly, the bed was made exactly the way Amber would have made it, with crisp white bedding and plump cushions – it certainly didn't look the way her bed had looked at home on the rare occasion when Jamie had reluctantly 'made the bed'.

Franc pulled her towards the edge of the bed and turned her to face him, "Remember Tresoro, nice and slowly, tonight is just for you. I want you to trust me."

Amber wasn't sure what 'just for you', meant but she did know that she was so ridiculously turned on that she wasn't altogether sure that she cared. Franc began to pull gently at the tie around her waist, holding her wrap-over dress. The dress opened easily at his touch and he slowly eased it from her shoulders, down her arms, until it landed in a pool at her feet. As Amber stood before him, naked except for her underwear which matched for once, she should have felt a lot more self-conscious than she did. Instead she felt only anticipation, excitement and arousal.

Franc viewed her with an appreciative gaze that made her feel more beautiful than she had in a long time. He held her at arm's length as he allowed his eyes to wander over her body; from her face, down her neck, to her breasts now shamelessly erect, to her stomach, to soft trimmed hair visible through her sheer knickers, down her thighs, to her feet still wearing the elegant nude court shoes that accentuated her slender calves. Even her feet seemed to warrant an appreciative gaze from Franc.

When he had taken his time to appreciate every last inch of her body he moved in closer to her to kiss her full lips. His tongue caressed and flickered over every inch of her mouth, lips and tongue before working its way down her neck where he licked and nibbled until she thought she could literally take no more. The experience was so intense she was helpless; she couldn't have left now if she had wanted to.

Gently he sat her down on the edge of the bed, kneeling on the floor between her legs. He continued to kiss her neck, working his way down towards her breasts where he teased her erect nipples between his teeth, pausing only to squeeze them between his thumb and forefingers whilst his mouth paid attention to her mouth once more. He reached down for her ankles lifting her gently up onto the bed so that she was laying on her back, her knees bent, her womanhood exposed before him. Franc began to trail his tongue from her ankles, up the inside of her left leg, her knee, towards her upper thigh, skimming briefly across her pussy. Amber moaned involuntarily and grabbed handfuls of the sheets in her fists as the sensations overwhelmed her. She was longing for him to thrust his tongue deep inside her wetness, but he did not. Instead he began the trail from ankle to thigh on her other leg. By the time he once again reached that sensitive place between her thighs, Amber was nigh on ready to come. Franc did not disappoint. With one placed under her buttocks lifting up towards his mouth, he used his other hand to gently caress her swollen clitoris. All the time his tongue licked and flicked around her wetness, nibbling the flesh on her thighs, replacing his fingers to gently suck on her. Each time she thought she was about to come, Franc would somehow sense her impending climax, holding back just enough to allow her to calm before bringing her again to the brink. Amber had never known intensity like it. She wanted to grab his hand and thrust it inside her, she wanted to scream at the top of her voice, grinding herself into his face. Just when she thought she could take no more, Franc drove his finger deep inside her and licked around and around her clit, not too fast, but not too slow until she came, crying out unintelligibly, fisting her hands into the sheets and she felt the pulsating waves of her orgasm. It felt like she came again and again, as waves of pleasure overtook and her body shuddered in sweet release.

Franc raised his head from between her thighs and pulled himself up onto the bed beside her. He stroked her hair and kissed her mouth gently as her orgasm subsided; muttering beautiful sweet nothings in Italian. Amber had never felt as alive as she did right then. The relaxation that overtook her then was euphoric and she gradually became re-aware of her surroundings, she began to feel a little embarrassed about the way she had totally let go.

She looked at Franc, "I'm sorry," she said.

"For what?" he asked. "It was beautiful."

"But what about you?" she asked almost shyly.

She hadn't given a moment's thought to his pleasure, so lost was she in her own – talk about a selfish lover!

"I told you; it is all for you tonight, only for you," replied Franc. "Besides, if you are not home by midnight your friend says she will cut off my man parts." Amber laughed at Freya's threats to Franc. She felt a little like a girl who had been to the sweet shop but was not allowed in. She'd had a taste of Franc and she knew without doubt that she wanted more.

Franc laughed as Amber pulled an exaggerated sad face.

"I want to make love to you, Tresoro, but I want you to trust me first. But for now, I can't promise to remain a gentleman if you stay." He lifted her from the bed and helped her back into her dress, pausing to kiss her more than once as he did so. He walked her back to her car and devoured her once more with his tongue before she sat down in the driver's seat. He looked back twice as he walked away from her car blowing her a kiss on the final time. Amber pulled out of the car park and drove back to Freya's in a stated of total euphoria.

Freya had flung the door open before Amber had a chance to put her key in the lock.

"Spill the beans!" she shrieked excitedly. "Was he as hot in the sack as he looks?"

"A lady never kisses and tells," laughed Amber, shrieking in mock pain as Freya dug her playfully in the ribs.

"I haven't waited until midnight on a school night for you to play all cagey with me," giggled Freya, "now dish the dirt, or I'll stop your wine rations!"

Freya went to the kitchen to fetch two glasses, filled with an ice cold Chardonnay, whilst Amber settled herself on the sofa. She had to admit she couldn't wait to share her gossip with her new friend. Amber hadn't felt this alive in ages, and like a pair of giggling school girls, Amber told while Freya mostly shrieked.

"He went down on you without a favour in return?" squeaked Freya. "I tell you, the man's a keeper!"

Amber knew deep down that Franc was anything but a keeper; sure he was charming and a total gentleman, not to mention drop dead gorgeous, but she really couldn't see them running off into the sunset together. He was a bo-ho artist who lived for today; he certainly didn't strike her as the 'becoming a stepdad to two stroppy teenagers' type. For a fleeting moment, she wondered what the hell Jamie would make of her current recklessness; but then he was busy parading his 'bits of stuff' right in front of her eyes (in the very place where she worked, no less!) so she didn't think he had much right to sit in judgement.

Amber resolved to put all thoughts of her battered marriage to one side for the time being and simply live in the moment. Jamie had made no further attempts to contact her and she imagined that he was waiting for her to make the first move in that cocky, self-assured way of his. In fact, the longer she left it, the more he was probably seething. Well he could fuck right off if he thought she was crawling back to him, begging for forgiveness for the very fact that he had behaved like a selfish arse for the past 'goodness-knows-how-long'! All in all, Amber felt pretty pleased that she had managed to finally find her own backbone, not to mention a little surprised!

It was one o'clock in the morning before the two friends finally calmed down enough to go to bed. Amber was very glad not to be on an early shift in the morning and it would make a change for her late-start morning not to be filled with housework, washing, cooking and shopping. The great thing about sharing with another woman was that they pretty much cleared up their own shit, instead of leaving it for the fairy to do. Freya also didn't demand tea on the table, nor did she expect Amber to wash her pants! Amber decided she would have a lie-in and read one of her books in bed, if only for an hour or so. Then she decided she would go and get her hair done before work. It would be nice to be self-indulgent for once. She was also very much looking forward to her meeting with the bank to discuss the business idea forming in her head.

Amber slept like a log that night, and her dreams were very racy! She dreamt of Franc, running his tongue up and down her inner thigh; remembering the moment when she had succumbed to the powerful sensation that overtook her whole being. When she awoke she felt ridiculously horny; she was like a bloody bitch in heat!

She did indeed enjoy a nice frothy coffee in bed with a good book and relished the peace and quiet – Freya had left early that morning for a jewellery making workshop in London and was due to be gone all day. She got up, showered and dressed, leaving her hair scrunched up in a loose bun as she had managed to get a hair appointment for lunchtime. She could have her hair done and bounce into work like 'the girl who just stepped out of a salon' on the hairspray advert!

She had almost choked on her breakfast at the text she had received from Franc – *Mmmm, deliciously naughty thoughts, remembering hearing you come xxx*

The butterflies she felt in both her stomach and her lady parts were difficult to ignore – God that man was sexy! With a sense of abandonment she had texted him back –

I can't remember it, I think you need to remind me xxx

Franc had replied immediately –

Come now! Xxx

Amber squirmed in her seat, almost giving in to his demands there and then! She replied –

Working, you'll have to wait, bad boy! Xx

Amber really didn't quite know who was replying to his texts – it certainly didn't feel like herself. She marvelled at the wanton, sex Goddess that seemed to have awoken inside her! Franc replied again -

Come for me after work xxx

Amber – *I think you mean come to me? Xx*

Franc – *I know what I meant xxx*

Amber felt she would be able to save him a job if he carried on texting her this seriously hot filth! She took only a few seconds to throw caution to the wind –

I will come to you and for you at 7 xx

She put her phone back in her bag before she could do any more damage, and also before she dissolved into a wet puddle on the kitchen floor!

Amber's trip to the hairdresser was both successful and liberating. She emerged with a new shoulder-length bob, having been brave enough to lose several inches from her long, albeit tatty and neglected hair. She had also dared to try a funky new fringe and a few bold slices of white blonde on the hairdresser's advice, which made her look fresher and younger than she had felt in years. She bounced out of the salon on cloud nine, excited at the prospect of seeing Franc later.

She half expected to see Jamie flouncing around by her make-up counter and she wasn't altogether whether she felt relieved or a tiny bit miffed that he had accepted their break up so readily. She wasn't oblivious enough to her own faults to realise what a hypocrite she was being in light of the fact that she was highly likely to be getting her brains bonked out in a few hours' time.

Mercifully, Amber's shift on a Friday was only a short one – 2 till 6 – after which she would have just enough time to pop indoors, quick wash and knicker change and some lippy and she'd be ready. Although – ready for what, she wondered? Amber had no doubt that tonight was most probably the night that she and Franc would do 'it'. She was physically ready, there was no doubt about that; every time she so much as thought about it she got a little quiver in her bits that caused her to flush with embarrassment. She was sure it was wrong on a quite a few levels to be practically getting off every 10 minutes whilst trying to advise on the benefits of the 'max length' as opposed to the 'extra volume' mascara. She was, however, undeniably nervous – what if she had forgotten how to do 'it'? She was pretty certain that 'it' wasn't altogether different whoever you were with; you placed part A into part B, wiggled about a bit and hey presto! But she didn't know if she was supposed to perform any particular tricks; what if Franc was used to more adventurous, not to mention younger, nubile conquests? She resolved to go with the flow and maybe a few drinks to loosen her up a bit; although if she got much 'looser' in her knicker region she'd have had her 'hey ho' moment long before part A got anywhere near part B!

When her shift ended, Amber stuffed the vile lilac tabard under the counter and nigh on ran through the door, barely pausing to say goodbye to the shop security guard. She drove home much faster than usual and ran indoors. Once she had washed, taking real care not to disturb her funky new hair, she changed, changed back, then changed again before she was happy with her outfit. She had decided against the jumpsuit (it would be tricky for Franc to slide his hand up her inner thigh if she was ensconced in what was essentially a giant Babygro), and finally settled on a silk shirt-dress in Chelsea blue that really complimented her blonde hair – besides, it was also easy to remove!

As she came down the stairs, her hands were shaking and her insides were doing a full 360 degrees. Freya walked in through the door and whistled as Amber reached the hallway, "Someone is definitely getting laid tonight! You look gorgeous, girlfriend!"

Amber's weak smile did little to disguise her nerves.

"What you need is a quick measure of Dutch courage," smiled Freya.

Amber followed Freya through to the kitchen, where Freya poured them both a glass of Prosecco.

"Knock him dead!" smiled Freya, raising her glass to toast Amber.

"I'm bricking it," laughed Amber, glugging gratefully at the cold bubbles.

"You'll be fine," said Freya, "just like riding a bike – or it will be for him anyway!"

Amber laughed and slapped her friend light-heartedly on the arm, "Cheeky cow!"

Amber glanced at the clock and drained her glass. It was 6.45pm; time to go!

"Wish me luck," she said. "I don't know when I'll be back."

"Have fun," said Freya, "I think we are fairly sure he's not an axe murderer by now – sex God maybe - but not an axe murderer!"

Amber hugged the friend that she now felt she had known for years rather than months. If nothing else had come out of joining the pottery class, then hot sex with an Italian sex god and a fantastic new best friend would do for her!

Amber's trembling fingers fumbled with the keys and she took a deep breath before climbing into her car. She drove the short journey to Franc's place, her mind racing.

Franc opened the door on her first knock, she smiled what she hoped was a confident, sex siren kind of a smile but feared she was fooling no-one, least of all herself.

Franc seemed to sense her nerves and took her by the hand, pulling her in towards him. He kissed her on the lips with those deliciously soft, full lips of his and Amber's nerves were instantly replaced with red hot desire.

He guided her into the kitchen area of the small cabin which was lit by what seemed like hundreds of candles. Soft music played in the background and Amber noticed an ice bucket on the kitchen table beside which stood two tall stemmed glasses and a vase containing the most beautiful bouquet of rich, blood red roses she had ever seen –this boy knew how to do romance! She wondered if he had secretly been reading her erotic novels –or, scarier still, maybe he could read her mind!

He poured something pink and bubbly into the glasses and handed one to Amber. They sipped at their drinks, never once taking their eyes from each other.

Amber relished the ice cold path of the decadently dry rose wine as it slid down her throat. Franc looked gorgeous in a white fitted t-shirt and low-waist, faded jeans; his feet were bare. He placed his glass on the table and stepped towards her. Amber's heart began to beat in her chest so hard that she was sure he could hear it. He placed a strong arm around her waist and pulled her assertively in towards him. The other hand he placed at the nape of her neck whilst he kissed her; probing her mouth with his tongue, teasing her lips apart until her own tongue found his. He licked and stroked and teased, biting her lip before kissing her so deeply, it was as if he were trying to possess every inch of her. Amber's arms hung loosely at her sides; one hand still clutching the wine glass. She was powerless in his arms, her body yielded to him of its own accord.

Something began to trickle down her leg and she realised that she had let the wine glass tilt to one side, spilling the remains of her drink. She edged herself towards the table, still joined to Franc, blindly feeling for the table to place her glass on it. Just at that moment, Franc moved his hand from the nape of her neck to caress her right breast, teasing the nipple between his thumb and forefinger, at which point Amber lost all control of her limbs. The glass fell to the floor, missing the edge of the table and shattering around their feet.

The unexpected noise momentarily interrupted their passionate embrace.

"Oh God, I'm sorry," said Amber, looking down at the shattered glass around Franc's bare feet. "Mind your feet, don't cut yourself!"

Franc did not reply, but instead swept Amber up into his arms and, taking one large stride across the broken glass, carried her towards the bedroom door, kicking it open with his foot. As he carried her across the threshold he began to kiss her again, and this time, free from the inconvenience of trying to hold on to a wine glass, Amber twisted her fingers into the dark curls at the base of his neck. A groan escaped his lips as she pulled at his hair.

"Are you ok, Tresoro?" asked Franc. "Are you sure?"

Amber knew exactly what he meant and responded with a breathy, "Yes." She had never wanted to be fucked as badly as she did right now, and she had *definitely* stopped worrying about her wobbly bits!

Franc laid her down on the bed. He pulled his t-shirt above his head revealing his beautifully tanned torso, a dark smattering of hair covered his chest trailing down to the waist of his jeans; he was perfect. He began to slowly unbutton Amber's shirtdress, taking his time to kiss each tiny patch of skin as it was revealed. Amber was bloody glad she hadn't opted for the jumpsuit!

Once he had removed her dress, he took time to admire her naked body, stroking her legs from ankle to thigh, gently skimming her throbbing pussy but never quite touching her there. Amber thought she may burst with desire. He kissed her neck, her shoulders, her breasts, her stomach, trailing his tongue over her sensitive flesh.

Finally, he slowly removed her knickers, hooking his thumbs into the delicate lace at the sides and pulling them slowly – almost torturously – down her legs and over her ankles. He looked down at her with hooded eyes, placing his middle finger in her mouth, pulling it in and out of her pursed lips, never taking his eyes from hers. Just when Amber thought she could take no more of his teasing, he plunged his now-wet finger deep into her. She literally almost came on the spot, tensing her legs in an attempt to delay her orgasm. He leaned back down over her, resuming his oral onslaught on her mouth, plunging his finger in and out of her, whilst his thumb caressed her clit. Amber came with a cry that was almost feral.

Franc stood and removed his jeans, revealing his cock that was now thick and hard.

"Are you sure, Tresoro?" he asked again. "It's ok, but you must tell me now, I'm not sure I could be a gentleman for too much longer."

Amber smiled and nodded her head, she was unable to speak but she knew she wanted him, and she certainly didn't want him to be any kind of gentleman on her account! Suddenly she realised that she did not have any kind of protection with her. It had been so long since she had needed any within her marriage and she wasn't taking any contraception.

She felt embarrassed at her lack of preparation. She opened her mouth to speak but she needn't have worried. Franc moved to the small bedside drawer and removed a silver packet. He tore open the packet and placed the condom slowly over his manhood. Amber inwardly breathed a sigh of relief – if she was honest she wasn't sure she could have resisted him with or without protection at this stage and she was glad that she hadn't had to make such a reckless decision.

Franc positioned himself above her; his long, strong legs either side of hers. He pulled her face towards his, kissing her deeply, his other hand holding hers. When he entered her, it was slow and gentle. He held still for a few moments gazing deeply into her eyes; her smile gave him the encouragement he needed and he began to grind into her – long deep strokes building in speed and strength. Amber lifted her legs and wrapped them around his waist, their fingers now entwined with each other's. Amber felt the pleasure building inside her. Her breathing quickened and she cried out unintelligible words. At that moment, Franc placed a hand under her behind and raised her hips so that he could fill her more deeply; this action caused Amber to practically explode around him and as her pussy pulsated around his gloriously hard cock, she felt his body stiffen as he came, buried deep inside her, his mouth finding hers once more, as he kissed her passionately while they both climbed down from their exquisite high.

They laid, still joined together for several minutes, before Franc rolled away from her, removing the condom and placing it in the bin beside the bed. Then, laying on his back, he pulled her into him so that she could rest her head on the soft hair covering his chest – it was a while before either of them spoke.

"I was worried about my wobbly bits," said Amber weakly.

"Your wobbly bits?" laughed Franc, raising an eyebrow. "Your wobbly bits are my absolute favourite!" and he jumped across her once more, jiggling her breasts in his hands.

Amber shrieked and made a mock attempt to escape his clutches, "Leave my wobbly bits alone!"

They had sex once more that evening; this time slower and less frenzied, but none the less knee-trembling. Franc brought her to orgasm with his tongue before making sweet, slow love to her.

Amber declined his offer to stay the night but was flattered that he had asked. She was glad he hadn't made her feel cheap. She made her way to the front door on decidedly jelly legs, her creased dress and just-shagged hair adding effect to her 'walk of shame' appearance.

Franc kissed her passionately one last time before she left and Amber drove home in a state of satisfied euphoria.

Freya had waited up for Amber, despite the late hour.

"Well? Spill the beans! Was he as good as he looks?" she asked eagerly.

"Better!" smiled Amber. "Sex on legs!"

The two friends giggled and laughed their way through a couple of late night brandies, with Amber feeling more and more like a school girl, regaling her first snog. Deep down she knew this thing with Franc was unlikely to go anywhere. He was an artist, a nomad. He travelled regularly; rarely stayed in one place for too long.

The Amber of only a few short weeks ago would have been frantically over-analysing the situation. Worrying about the lack of permanence, where the 'relationship' was going. What would happen tomorrow, or next week or next month? The new and improved Amber had decided that she had taken the safe route for far too long – coasting along in her easy but boring job, taking the path of least resistance in her marriage. Amber had resolved that, whatever the outcome, she was going to put herself first for a change –take charge of her own destiny instead of constantly making excuses….and of course have a little fun along the way!

She had begun to form an idea for her new business, making small trinket boxes out of clay. At the moment, even if it never grew into anything more than a hobby, a cathartic way to spend her time whilst satisfying her creative desires; when she worked, Amber found a peace that she not felt in a long time – if ever. She had begun to play around with a few designs at Freya's kitchen table in the times when she wasn't at work. Freya had been impressed with her creativity – she had a real flair for the tiny, intricate, pots and dishes that she had produced. The boxes were delicate in their construction, painted with beautifully dainty designs; some with tiny gemstones sunk into the clay. Amber's idea was for them to hold tiny, but precious objects such as a child's first tooth, or a lock of hair – items which although of no monetary value were often priceless to the owner. She was however, still struggling to find a suitable name for her 'business' – such as it currently was.

After their third, rather generous brandy, Amber told Freya that she really thought it was time for bed. She could feel her hangover arriving already, which was never a good sign! They climbed the stairs to bed, and Amber fell gratefully into the freshly laundered sheets in the little guest room in which she felt so at home. It was only moments before she fell into a very deep sleep, dreaming of the delicious Franc. Amber was awoken from her deep sleep by the sound of buzzing on her bedside table. She woke with a start, fumbling around for the light switch in order to locate her phone. Her heart was pounding in her chest; she had always hated late night calls, in her mind they were always the result of bad or unwelcome news. She finally grabbed hold of her phone, catching a glimpse of the time as she did so – 3.17am. Now she was really panicking; who on earth would call her at this time of the morning? She didn't even bother to check the caller display in her eagerness to connect the call.

"Hello? Mrs Truelove? This is the Queen Elizabeth Hospital in Norwich. Please don't be alarmed."

A million thoughts raced through Amber's mind – not least the sheer alarm she felt at the caller's very insistence that she do the exact opposite! She didn't know anyone in Norwich.

"Hello, what is it? What's wrong?" replied Amber

sitting up straight in bed trying to calm her nerves.

"It's ok, Mrs Truelove, please don't be alarmed. I am calling from the Queen Elizabeth. We have your daughter Holly with us. She's ok, but she has had a bit of an accident. A couple of broken bones, but nothing that can't be mended."

"Oh my God, Holly!" cried Amber. "But Holly isn't in Norwich! Where is she? Is she ok?"

Amber's words came out in a rush, interspersed by barely concealed sobs. The absolute dread that every mother feels on hearing that their child was hurt was coursing its way through Amber's every nerve.

At the moment, Amber's bedroom door opened and Freya entered, having heard Amber's frantic voice. She sat down on Amber's bed and carefully took the phone from Amber's shaking hand.

"Yes, this is Mrs Truelove's friend, I'm afraid she's in shock. Perhaps you could explain it to me?" said Freya calmly.

As Freya listened to the nurse on the phone she put her arm around Amber's shoulders, holding her tightly. She nodded and made little noises of recognition as she listened carefully to the details being given to her. At one point she reached into the bedside cabinet and pulled out a small pad and a pen, scribbling down a few notes.

When she had hung up the phone, Freya hugged Amber tightly and reassured her that everything was fine. It seemed that Holly and a few friends had travelled to Norwich for some kind of concert. They were out enjoying the evening, as youngsters are supposed to do, when Holly had stepped into the road to cross over, not noticing the push bike weaving in and out of the traffic at breakneck speed. She had been knocked over with quite some force and, thankfully, her friends had immediately called an ambulance. She was now in the hospital suffering from concussion, a nasty black eye, two broken fingers and a broken wrist. She was bruised and sore, but stable and a lot more comfortable thanks to a dose of morphine and some carefully applied bandaging.

Amber hugged her friend tightly, thanking her for taking charge of the situation and writing down the details in a far more coherent manner than she had been capable of a few minutes ago. She was so relieved that Holly was alive and not in danger, but she was anxious to get to her as soon possible.

"I have to go, of course," said Amber. "I need to tell Jamie."

"Just do what you've got to do, babe. I'll phone your work tomorrow and tell them what's happened. Don't worry about anything, she'll be fine," said Freya kindly.

"Thank you," Amber replied, "I really don't know what I'd have done without you. Not just today but the last few weeks, your friendship means a lot to me," Amber's voice began to crack as she spoke.

"Don't be daft," said Freya. "I needed a new friend anyway! Now get yourself ready and call Jamie. I'll make us a coffee while we wait. I suppose he'll pick you up? You can't really drive."

"Oh I hadn't thought of that," said Amber. "I'll just ring and see what he says."

Amber felt nervous as she rang Jamie's phone. They hadn't spoken at all in weeks, and not properly for years if the truth be known. He picked after a few rings, his voice croaky with sleep.

"Amber, what's up? You ok?"

Amber felt quite heartened that he still seemed to care about her welfare, if only a little, but then it would have been pretty shitty if he hadn't given a toss after twenty years! She repeated the story as calmly as she could, asking him if he would come with her.

"Of course, I'll bloody come," he said, not unkindly. "Text me the postcode and I'll be there in 20…and don't worry I haven't been drinking."

"Thanks Jamie," said Amber, a little surprised that he

hadn't been drinking on what used to be his pool night – she was glad she hadn't had to make excuses as to why she wasn't able to drive, either!

Sure enough, Jamie arrived 20 minutes later, banging softly on the front door in a bid to not disturb Freya's neighbours any more than necessary. The girls had been waiting for him in the kitchen, drinking a hot black coffee and saying very little. Amber's mind was totally preoccupied with her daughter's well-being – she would always be her baby girl.

Amber opened the door when Jamie knocked. He looked different somehow – like he had lost weight. He was unshaven and his eyes were still puffy from sleep. He smiled politely in Freya's direction, thanking her for looking after Amber. Amber was surprised by this gesture from her once-aloof husband where her friends were concerned.

"You ready?" he asked Amber.

"As I'll ever be," smiled Amber weakly; quite frankly her nerves were shattered and she felt sick with worry despite knowing that Holly was safe.

"She'll be ok," said Jamie, squeezing her hand.

Amber squeezed his hand back and blinked away the tears. They said their goodbyes to Freya and made their way in silence to the car.

The journey to Norwich was a long one, but the roads were quiet, thanks to the early morning hour. They travelled for most of the way in silence – Jamie paying careful attention to the road – Amber's mind racing with thoughts of her daughter. Little memories from her childhood kept popping in to Amber's mind, reminding her of just how much she loved her and of the relief she felt that she hadn't lost her.

"We need to phone Dan," said Amber suddenly, guilty that she hadn't thought of this sooner.

"It's ok," said Jamie, "we can phone him later. There's no point waking him in the middle of the night and scaring the life out of him. We'll phone him as soon as he's likely to be awake."

"That'll be about midday then," laughed Amber, feeling relieved to have something to smile about.

They both chuckled, no doubt having similar thoughts about their son's reluctance to get out of bed from the day he was born. Amber remembered the daily battle to get him up and out – even when he was in sixth form, she would put a cup of tea on his bedside table, run him a bath, then practically drag him out of bed and throw him into it after shouting at him to wake up at least a hundred times! That boy had always loved his sleep.

Amber and Jamie continued their journey in companionable silence; she glimpsed him a few times from the side as he drove. He had definitely lost weight, his face looked drawn, he looked like someone who hadn't slept all that well – not just from tonight. She noticed the smattering of grey hair around his hairline and the rough shadow of his unshaven chin. He still looked familiar to her, but different at the same time. Maybe that's just what happened when you took a step back from someone you'd spent every day with for the last twenty years; maybe you just saw them in a new light.

They arrived at the hospital and walked quickly and purposefully to the reception desk. Amber's heart was beating wildly in her chest and her hands were clammy. The security guy on reception directed them to the Accident and Emergency ward and they made their way there almost at a run.

As soon as Amber entered one of the small wards to the side of the A&E waiting room, she saw her precious daughter; propped up in a bed, her eyes swollen and bruised, a large dressing covering a cut on her head. Her right arm was in a sling and the fingers on her left hand were heavily bandaged.

Amber covered her mouth to stop herself from crying out. She rushed over to Holly's bedside with Jamie close behind. She tried to carefully hold her daughter's hand, mindful of the fact that she was probably very sore. Holly opened her eyes as she felt her Mum's presence. She gave a weak smile.

"Oh baby. Thank God you're alive," said Amber, tearfully.

"I'm ok Mum, really, just a bit sore," said Holly, wincing as she pulled herself up in the bed.

Jamie moved in behind Amber and put his arm around her to comfort her – it felt a little strange but not unwelcome.

"You ok, love?" he asked, his voice weary from worry and the long drive on little sleep.

"I'm fine Dad, honestly," replied Holly.

The sun was starting to rise as it was now gone 7 in the morning. Amber sat beside Holly's bed, doing her best to hold her hand, while Holly dozed. She was tired and shaken from her accident, not mention a little sore, but at least she was safe and in the best place.

Jamie sat on the other side of the bed, struggling to keep his eyes open as he watched his daughter and wife. Eventually he got up and went to the cafeteria to get them both a coffee. He returned with two steaming hot cups of coffee – it was not lost on Amber that he had remembered to buy her a cappuccino, which was her absolute favourite.

A little while after, the doctor came around and spoke to Amber and Jamie. They would be keeping Holly in for another 24 hours, just to keep her under observation, after which she was free to go home. Amber wondered exactly where 'home' might be for all of them – but Holly was blissfully unaware of the state her parents' marriage was in and Amber certainly wasn't going to do anything to rock the boat at this stage.

Once they had spoken to the doctor, Jamie beckoned Amber to one side, away from Holly's earshot.

"Look Amber, we both need to get some sleep, we'll be of no use to Holly tomorrow if we don't rest, and I certainly can't drive when I'm this knackered. I took the liberty of booking a hotel nearby – we can get a shower, a bit of sleep and come back again later. We could probably do with something to eat too."

The look on Amber's face must have told a thousand tales because he quickly added, "Don't worry I've booked separate rooms, I understand you're not up for sharing with me right now."

Amber breathed a sigh of relief. She wasn't sure how she felt about sharing a room with Jamie, especially when she was not long out of the bed of another man – an event that now seemed a lifetime ago. She certainly wasn't ready for happy families, although strangely enough she bore him no malice.

She nodded her agreement to him. They returned to their daughter who was now sleeping soundly. Amber left her a little note beside her bed, telling her that they would back for tea time visiting and that they loved her.

They left the hospital, the lack of sleep and the stress of the night time's drama really beginning to take its toll. Amber was suddenly grateful for Jamie's practical thinking. They had a breakfast at the hotel and Amber couldn't remember ever enjoying tea and toast so much – it seems they had both been starving.

After breakfast, it was a little awkward as they made their way to their separate rooms, nodding an overly formal goodnight to each other – although not as awkward as sharing a room would have been. Amber was grateful and surprised by Jamie's tactfulness – it wasn't a trait he had shown much of late.

Once in her room, Amber ran herself a deep, hot bath and sank gratefully into the soothing bubbles. She dried herself using one of the hotel's impossibly thick towels, before wrapping herself in a dressing gown and laying on top of the bed. She was warm and comfortable and she fell asleep in seconds.

Amber woke to hear a soft knocking on the door. She

glanced at the clock and realised she had slept for almost 5 hours! She padded across the thick carpet and opened the door cautiously. Jamie stood in the doorway, clean shaven and obviously showered. He looked fresher and much better rested than he had this morning.

"Hi," he said. Amber noticed that he seemed nervous.

"Hi," said Amber, "good sleep?"

"Much better," he smiled. "Look Amber, I know we need to talk, and I know today isn't really the time….but I just wanted to say that I do know I've been an arse."

"Oh," said Amber, genuinely surprised by his frankness. "Well yes, you have been quite a bit of an arse actually."

"I know. And for what it's worth: I'm sorry. I've missed you, Amber."

"I don't really know what to say Jamie, if I'm honest," said Amber.

"I know," he sighed. "I get it; really I do. Like I said, today isn't really the day, but maybe we could get some lunch and at least be a bit civil to each other before we go back to our daughter?"

"That sounds great," said Amber, with genuine relief.

"And if Holly has to come home for a while, I can always have a job away from home for a bit if that helps," he said tentatively.

Amber was touched by his attempt to put her at ease; to not force her into a situation where they were thrown back into living together after their recent separation.

"I'd appreciate that, Jamie, thank you," replied Amber. "I'm not sure how I feel about things right now and I don't think I can play happy families just at the moment. But thank you; I mean that."

Jamie sighed, "I know Amber, I know. I'll meet you in the bar downstairs."

And, with that, he disappeared down the hall way, his shoulders hunched, hands in his pockets. Amber almost felt sorry for him, but she owed it to herself to stay strong.

She needed time to work out in her own mind how she felt about things; her marriage, her feelings towards Jamie, Franc – about her desire for change.

Half an hour later, Amber joined Jamie for lunch in the bar. They chatted about this and that, about the kids, work – Amber even told him about her recent creative venture. The Jamie she knew would, she imagined, have dismissed such a venture out of hand as a frivolous waste of time, but he actually seemed interested. For the first time in so long, she felt that he was actually interested in what she had to say and she had to admit to herself that it felt good. They did not mention their earlier conversation, nor did they talk about their marriage – at all – and Amber was grateful for that. She was not ready to deal with that right now.

They phoned Daniel who had been out diving off some coral reef, in some far flung corner of the globe. Amber told him at least 20 times to stay safe, and she chided him gently for laughing at her 'over-worrying' as he put it. He had been concerned about his sister, but quickly recovered as soon as he knew she was ok; in the way only the carefree youth are able.

When they returned to the hospital, Holly seemed brighter and well rested and they were both mighty relieved. It was decided that she would go back to her student digs and that Amber would stay with her for a few days. Amber had been very relieved at this suggestion - it would save all the awkwardness of returning to the family home – but she was sure Jamie had seemed a little disappointed although he said nothing.

Jamie had driven them back to Holly's digs and kissed them both on the cheek when he left. It was strange for Amber – an intimate gesture by the man from whom she had been so distant.

Within a couple of days, Holly was back to her usual bubbly self, having been well-fed on some of Amber's home cooking. Her room mates had been mighty glad of

Amber's culinary offerings and took full advantage – probably before returning to their usual student diet of Super Noodles and beans on toast. Amber had cleaned the house from top to bottom and tried hard to ignore the fact that the kitchen floor probably hadn't been washed since they had moved in last year! Holly's arm was now in plaster, so she was safe to move about and return to uni. Amber had much enjoyed spending time with her daughter although she couldn't deny she would be pleased to return home – if nothing else the music they listened to was driving her up the wall!

She caught the train back home and Freya came to collect her from the station. Amber was pleased to see her friend and they hugged each other tightly. She had worried about going back to Freya's house – she didn't want to outstay her welcome – but Freya told her not to be so bloody stupid; she loved having her there.

Life returned pretty much to normal, although Amber was fully aware of just how far removed her new 'normal' was from her old life. She returned to her shifts on the make-up counter and continued to make her trinket boxes and keepsake dishes in Freya's kitchen. The more she made, the more ideas she had, and she now had a sizeable collection. Freya encouraged her to participate in local craft fairs, alongside her jewellery stall, and Amber was beginning to sell and take orders with increasing regularity.

Jamie had texted her a few times since their return, asking if she would like to meet him for a drink and she had replied saying that she would when she felt ready. It wasn't that she wanted to string him along; just that she didn't to slip back into her old life. She was happier now than she had ever been and much more content with herself.

She continued to see Franc now and again and, although the sex was truly amazing, she was now surer than ever that they were not right for each other in the long term. How terribly bohemian she felt, having casual but hot sex with an Italian god, knowing that she was not committed in any way and knowing that, when it did end, there would be absolutely no hard feelings on either side.

It was about a fortnight after Holly's accident when things did in fact end between her and Franc. She had visited his cabin after pottery class, having been seduced in the usual way, with candle light and champagne, and the best cunnilingus this side of heaven, when he announced that he had a commission for an art gallery in Milan. Bless his heart, he even asked her to go with him and, whilst the prospect of lying on an Italian beach gazing up at a cloudless blue sky whilst Franc did something entirely naughty with sun cream was not totally unappealing, Amber knew that this was where their liaison would end. As she had predicted, there were no tears on either side, just a gloriously, pleasurable goodbye shag, and the genuine wish for each other's continued happiness.

If nothing else, Franc had taught Amber how a lady should be treated. He had taught her to be shamelessly unafraid to seek her own pleasure, and he had even taught her to be proud of her 'wobbly bits'!

Strangely enough, Amber felt no guilt about her affair with Franc; she really felt that it was fate and, without it, she would have never learned how to pursue her own happiness. She realised, also, that she had put off Jamie until things had ended properly with Franc. She was not sure how things were going to pan out with Jamie, but she needed to draw a line under one situation before she could fully embrace another. She had absolutely no intention of telling Jamie about Franc – regardless of how things worked out – but she was not a cheater.

Amber and Jamie met at a local pub and, surprisingly, the conversation flowed pretty well. She had been apprehensive, but needn't have worried. Jamie looked great. He was wearing dark jeans and a fitted shirt that showed off his new, slimmer physique – losing a few pounds actually suited him. He was clean shaven and his hair had been freshly cut; Amber was touched that he had made an obvious effort.

He held the door open for her when they left (something he had never done before), went to the bar for their drinks and put her favourite tunes on the juke box – little things that only someone who knows you well can do. When the evening came to a close, he asked her if she would like to come home for coffee. Amber declined. She was not ready for such an encounter just yet, although she definitely liked the new, more considerate Jamie. It wasn't that he was being false or over-the-top cheesy; he just wasn't being a selfish, ignorant wanker any more.

They continued to see each other a few times and, finally, Amber agreed to go home for coffee. It felt strange to enter the home that they had shared for so many years and she almost felt like a stranger. Jamie had taken her hand as he sensed her awkwardness.

"I know it feels a bit weird for you, babe, but for me it feels so good to have you home. I've been miserable without you," he said.

"What about your girlfriend?" asked Amber, referring to the girl she had seen him with in the department store that time. Inwardly she had kicked herself for asking – knowing what a giant hypocrite she was being when she had been having her brains shagged out on a regular basis by Franc the Italian sex god – but curiosity had got the better of her.

Jamie had laughed, "She was a mate's girlfriend from work. I was being a twat and trying to make you jealous – didn't really work, did it?"

"Not really," laughed Amber, "I just thought you were being a cocky twat!"

"Well, you got that right," Jamie replied. "I've been such an arsehole, Amber. I've totally taken you for granted. If you don't want to live here anymore, we could move. I want to make this work."

"I'm not prepared to go back to how things were," said

Amber. "I wasn't happy."

"I will prove it, babe. We'll have fun again; like we used to. You don't have to move back in straight away. Whenever you're ready," he said, almost pleading with her.

Later that night, when they made love, Amber was surprised to find that there was none of the awkwardness she had been worried about. Her new found confidence in her own body gave her the freedom to relax and enjoy the moment. She realised that she had played her own part in the decay of their marriage. She had not been honest about how she felt and her almost pathological need to avoid a confrontation of any kind had led her to be little more than apathetic. In truth, she hadn't really fought for their marriage either.

When they lay in each other's arms they *really* talked, for what was probably the first time in years. The night seemed to last forever but also disappear in moments. They later referred to that night as, 'the shortest, longest night'.

Amber returned to Freya's house, wanting to take things slowly with Jamie. In truth she wanted him to fight for her, if only a little bit – to put his money where his mouth was, so to speak. They continued to go out on dates to the cinema, nice restaurants, country pubs and Sunday afternoon walks – in short they grew to like each other again, let alone love each other.

Amber continued to make her clay trinket boxes and had added some of her range to her Facebook page – something which Freya had helped her with and something which her kids couldn't believe she had mastered.

It was a Saturday afternoon when Jamie texted her. They hadn't been due to meet until the evening and she was looking forward to it. He had been a little mysterious the last few days and she hadn't been back to the house since Wednesday; she hoped that nothing was amiss.

Hey, babe, know we've got a date later but can you spare me half an hour?

Amber replied, *Course. Everything ok?*

You'll see ♥♥

It tickled Amber how Jamie had taken to using emojis in his texts; seems he was joining the techno revolution along with her. It was kind of sweet, really, considering this was a bloke who barely put a kiss on a message before – it was a further sign that he was actually making a bit of an effort. Amber had come to realise that, despite her love of romantic fiction, she didn't really need grand gestures or flamboyant declarations of love. Sure, the odd helicopter trip to Paris might have been nice, but billionaires were a little bit thin on the ground in reality!

Thirty minutes later, Freya's doorbell rang and Amber opened it to Jamie. He was grinning like a Cheshire cat but remaining annoyingly tight-lipped when she tried to quiz him about what he was up to. She was surprised when she realised he was simply driving her to their house – she wondered if he only needed her to help with washing machine!

He opened the door and took her hand, leading her up the front path. He guided her up the stairs and stood her outside the spare bedroom which had always been used as an office.

"Now, close your eyes," he said cryptically.

"What the bloody hell are you up to?" asked Amber.

"Just stop nattering and do as you're told for once, woman!" laughed Jamie.

Amber slapped him playfully on his arm but did as she was told – she made a mental note not to make a habit of it!

Once she had her hands over her eyes, Jamie opened the door and led her into the room.

"Open," he said.

Amber opened her eyes and was so gobsmacked by what she saw, she thought she might cry. The whole room had been completely transformed. A large work desk stood in the corner, above which long shelves lined the wall. The carpet had been replaced with practical wooden boards and a comfortable chair sat in front of the desk. What struck Amber the most was the way in which the room had been decorated – turquoise blue walls, a beautiful blind in turquoise and cerise pink stripes and a patchwork cushion in pinks and oranges sat on the chair. On one of the walls was a collection of unique and beautiful frames each containing photos of family memories – a trip to the seaside when the kids were small, a Christmas morning and, more recently, a photo of her and Jamie at a restaurant holding hands and smiling for the camera.

Amber looked at Jamie, utterly lost for words.

"I thought you could use this as your work room. If you don't like it, it's ok. Freya said you liked these colours…." his voice trailed off nervously.

"Oh Jamie, it's fabulous, I love it. And I *do* love the colours; I was just a bit surprised that you chose them!" laughed Amber.

"Yeah well, if it had been up to me you'd have got magnolia," laughed Jamie. "Like I said, Freya helped me quite a bit. She's actually really nice, I'm glad you've found a friend just for you."

Amber might have previously thought his comment about finding a friend to be patronising but she knew he was genuine. He truly wanted her to be happy and that meant more to her than anything.

"Your stuff's really good Amber; give up your crappy job and follow your dream. I'll support you all the way," said Jamie, squeezing her hand.

Amber felt the tears well in her eyes. This was better than any bottle of champagne or bunch of roses. This had come from the heart. It had taken effort – not money – but effort. Jamie had clearly spent time thinking about what she would want, asking Freya for her advice, wanting to get it just right – this was true love.

"One more thing," said Jamie. "If you don't like the

name you can change it..."

Amber looked at him curiously. Jamie pulled a long flat package from behind the door, wrapped in brown paper. Amber ripped off the paper and studied the contents.

It was a wooden sign. It was beautifully signwritten with the words 'TrueLove Memories.'

"I thought it would be a good name for your business,' said Jamie shyly. "But you don't have to keep it."

"Jamie, it's perfect," whispered Amber, tears now running freely down her face.

"Well, don't look so bloody cheerful about it," joked Jamie. "If I'd known you were going to ball your eyes out, I wouldn't have spent the last three nights decorating till 2 in the morning!"

Amber threw her arms around her husband, and right then she knew that things would be ok. The path to true love had not run smooth, for sure, but she wouldn't have changed a thing.

"I love you," she said, planting a kiss on his lips. "And thank you. It's the sweetest thing you could possibly have done."

"Thank God for that," sighed Jamie, the relief clear on his face. "Now will you *please* come home?!"

"I'll have to now," laughed Amber, "I've got a business to run!"

THANK YOU!

To my Reader:

Many thanks for buying *The Path to True Love,* I hope you enjoyed reading it.

If you did enjoy it, please post a review at Amazon, Goodreads or your favourite social network site and let your friends know about *The Path to True Love.*

Happy Reading!
All the best
Karen

CONTACT DETAILS

Website: writesmarteducation.co.uk

Follow on twitter: twitter.com/kaz0789

Cover Design by www.StunningBookCovers.com

Published by: Raven Crest Books:
ravencrestbooks.com

Like us on Facebook:
facebook.com/ravencrestbooksclub

27916724R00050

Printed in Great Britain
by Amazon